No Known Relatives

Brigid O'Connor

For anyone who's secret was never shared and memories were never cherished.

This is for you.

PROLOGUE

1984

Crouch down low, ignore what's on the ground, broken
bottles and used condoms. It's cold down here. Wipe that
thought out of your head. Nee naw nee naw. Here's the
ambulance. Peek over the balcony. Slow. Slow. Don't draw
attention to yourself. Remember what Mam said. 'Don't call
me Mam. Makes me sound ancient'. OK Lizzy it is. Be OK.
Don't be dead. There's a sound of a football. Brazil vs
Germany. They've been there all summer. Just stopping
for crisps. And a look up girls' skirts. The ambulance has
stopped. I can see into our hall. Lizzy's Spanish lady with
the maracas is peeping out, her bun immaculate. One of
the ambulance men knocks her over. The World Cup final
has stopped below. The boys climb up the steps to reach
our flat. They sit on the wall, and I hunker down lower.
They open their crisps, girl's skirts forgotten today. 'Thin
Lizzy's knackered', the chunkiest boy says. I blush for her
sake. She hates that name, nothing to do with the band
that she loves. 'I'd marry Phil Lynott in a heartbeat', she's
said so many times. As if it was possible. 'You got to live

your life like everything's possible', she always says. Thin Lizzy with her love of booze, prescription pills and anything anyone can find for her. She wanted to be a dancer and fall into a man's arms. She loves a well-dressed man with a scent of cologne. She has a man's handkerchief in a drawer with an old-fashioned scent on it and I've always imagined it's my dad's scent – masculine, spicy and long-faded. The boys are getting excited. I peek over again. There she is, lying on a stretcher, bruised, and tarnished and trying to put on her lipstick. She's got bruises everywhere. The other night, when she slept on the chair, I put some cream on them. She has varicose veins that somehow look like the map of the London Underground which one of my 'uncles' brought home from London for me. She always wanted to go to London. 'Go to the West End with a classy bloke', she said. But there she is on her stretcher. Anna told me they won't let her out this time. 'Too much booze and pills and the flat's a kip', she said. I try to dust it so the council won't take it back, but sometimes when I listen to my records, I forget. She's sitting up on the stretcher. Flirting with the ambulance man. Drink soaked, pill popping Lizzy with cheap bleach in her thinning hair, lipstick applied to half her lips and a map of London on her legs. Still like Rapunzel. Thinking a man is going to rescue her. Poor old Mam. The ambulance man asks her a question. The boys are laughing and pointing at her. My heartbeat gets faster. Breathe. 'Is there anyone I should call, love?', he asks her, the word 'love' brings a tear to her eyes. Lizzy looks around, searching for me. She sighs, leans into the ambulance man, and says, 'No-one, no, no-one at all'. I stay till the ambulance is long gone. The World cup game is back on. I stay till Anna finds me. And him. 'Can I stay with you, Anna?', I ask. She's not happy. I stand up to face them. My legs are shaky, and I wobble a little. I trip and fall against the man. He smiles, nicotine-coloured teeth and indoor skin. The sun comes out, my dress becomes transparent. The man holds me tight. 'Course she can stay with us, Anna. A lovely girl like her. I'm sure we can find something for her to do'. Anna's not pleased but wants to keep her man. She fixes the strap on her red high heels, grimacing as the bunions on her feet hurt her. Red heels and red lipstick. This man is important to her. A keeper, maybe. Lizzy and Anna are always looking for a keeper. 'Follow me, so', she says. Clippity clop in her cheap high heels, her hand firmly around the waist of her new man. 'I'll be so quiet, Anna. You won't know I'm here'. I take one last look at our flat. Bye, Lizzy. I never see her again.

CHAPTER 1

2009

MARTHA:

Dad believes that I seek Mum in every worn hand I hold, in every wheelchair I wheel. Maybe he's right. But she is gone. Dad plays piano solo now as Mum isn't here to sing along to his performances. When the sun shines into the music room, dust floats in the air around him. I fool myself and imagine it is her, attempting to rearrange the atoms so she may return to us. Dust has replaced her. Dad's hands shake while he plays, but the important thing is that he keeps playing. Resilience is everything. Conor carries my mother's spirit. He remains kind, despite the childish taunting he suffers at 'The View' Nursing Home. Some of the staff call him a weirdo and a loner just because he doesn't like their company. When you reject people, they like to put you in a box of their own design, their tainted image of you adorning it.

It started for me when I watched Conor with Peter in the garden. Love can find you anytime, anywhere. They needed a nurse present for their trip to the 'nicotine' tree and I volunteered. I was curious about the young and attractive care assistant who lives in a fairy-tale cottage on the grounds. Conor wheeled Peter through the garden, and we displaced cherry blossom petals as we rushed through the trees. Conor sang 'Born to be Wild' and Peter laughed so hard, that I thought he might lose his breath. He was fine, just living in the moment and feeling air rushing through the sparse bit of hair he had left. I like brushing Peter's hair at night. He smiles and says,

"Well Martha, what would the ladies think? Would I get a dance?".

"Of course, you would", I reply. He smiles then, not quite believing me, but wanting to.

We arrived at the back of the garden and Conor lifted Peter gently from the wheelchair and placed him under an oak tree. He took out the cigarettes, gave one to Peter and they settled down to smoke, the oak tree absorbing some of the nicotine. Conor pressed play on his iPod and put the earbuds into Peter's ears, played Metallica by mistake and Peter jumped out of his skin and apologised to me for saying 'Jesus Christ!'. Conor changed the track and Peter smiled and said 'Sea Sounds' as he listened to the sound of breaking waves. He started talking then and I could see by the way Conor spoke the words quietly to himself that he had heard the story many times before. Peter smiled as

5

he spoke,

"My mother used to take us out to the beach, the first chance of a bit of sun. We'd spend all day, me and my brother on the sand and we used to cry when it was time to leave. She used to say, well that was great, but it's time to go home now and she'd put cream on my burnt shoulders and say, "Well, Peter, wasn't that the best day ever?".

A tear travelled down his cheek. Conor and I tried to wipe it away at the same time. Our fingers connected and he looked right at me, the two of us dusted in petals like a bride and groom. I saw the tattoo on his arm then, "veritatem voluntas ex' and I was just about to ask what it meant when the dinner bell could be heard, and the spell was broken.

"Mince time", Peter said. We returned to the nursing home, subdued and wheeling Peter in his wheelchair. He had fallen asleep by the time we left the garden. Conor asked me my name as we lifted Peter into his seat in the dining room. "Martha", I said in what I thought was a husky, flirtatious tone, but somehow sounded like I was at the start of a throat infection.

"It's a really pretty name", he said, and I blushed. The world has a peculiar way of sending Cupid to visit. Between the garden and the dining room, love had wandered casually into my life.

CHAPTER 2

ANGELA:

I am standing at the dining table in my plush, suburban Dublin home. I set two sophisticated place settings. I pick up my mobile phone, dial a number and speak seductively to my husband, Matthew. I ask him if he received my text earlier. He replies that he did, but as he is in work, he CANNOT (he definitely said cannot in capital letters) just race home because I am ovulating. I frown and walk up the stairs as I talk on the phone. I put the phone on speaker and place it on top of a chest of drawers in my stylishly decorated bedroom. Everything in my house has a word or two prefixing it; stylishly decorated, carefully appointed, south facing. Affluence is all about prefixes. I remove some tiny underwear from a drawer. I tell Matthew that I will make it worth his while and give him a menu of lingerie to choose from. He is scathing just as I get to whale-boned corset and tells me that I am getting obsessive and boring. I drop the seductive routine. I order Matthew to get home and make me pregnant. As he argues with me, I switch the phone off and walk to another room. We revel in phone cutting off, us designer-clad pair. We play it like an elaborate game of chess. I open a wardrobe door, look at a row of baby clothes hanging in it and sit on the floor of the Normandy-sourced unit. I pick up a bottle of baby talc, pour some on the back of my hand, inhale the scent and smile.

Later, I'm preparing dinner in my 'Shaker with a twist' kitchen. An elderly well-dressed couple, my parents-in-law, talk to me, or at me, depending on the viewpoint. In the window reflection, I watch my mother-in-law, Clare, touch various surfaces with her finger, checking for dust. I often think that Clare should have been a cleaning products sales specialist. Or a forensic pathologist. My father-in-law, Paul, touches walls and remarks on how 'sound' they are. I sigh and continue to prepare salad. Clare says that I am such a lucky lady to have a wonderful house in the right neighbourhood. The right neighbourhood is Clare's religion. She tells me that that I need some babies to brighten up the house, as if babies are home accessories and that I could just pick them up in the lighting section in IKEA, put them in a bag and wander off for some Swedish meatballs. I wash hard-boiled eggs in the sink. Outside, a workman, Luke, packs up for the day. He walks into the kitchen, trailing mud. I've always had a bit of a thing for a man who trails mud. Clare looks at him suspiciously. She's oblivious to mud trailing men. There is an awkward silence.

I turn to my in-laws and in a hostess tone tell them to go through to the sitting room and that I'll bring them through their sherries. Clare flinches when I say, 'sitting room', preferring me to use the word 'lounge' which is the proper word for the room people sit in, in her world full of beige ladies. Clare is reluctant to leave. Paul puts his arm around her and leads her out of the room, like a horse at Fairyhouse racecourse.

Luke closes the door with his foot and pulls me towards him. I feign pushing him away, but then lean into him, smelling skin and salt. Luke strokes my hair and tells me that he knows I want him. I can hazard a guess that he says this to every woman and know that he is a walking cliché, but I refuse to register this information.

I kiss him back, hard. I check myself, change my mind, walk to the back door, and open it. I wait for Luke to say, "You'll be back for more, love".

Three seconds later, he leans in close and there it is – "You'll be back for more, sweetheart".

O.K. the sweetheart was off script. Luke leaves, smiling. A trail of his saliva trickles down the side of my face and into my mouth. I lick my lips and shiver. I walk to the sink, pick up my largest knife and with great force, cut a hard-boiled egg in half.

I call my in-laws through to dinner and say all the right things about candles and linen napkins flown from Italy to grace my table. Clare is slightly mollified. We eat dinner in the candlelit dining room. Clare drones on about how it's a pity that Matthew is in London and how it is tragic that I have no children to keep me occupied. I look out the window, suddenly craving salted skin. Clare persists in reminding me that I am not getting any younger. I jump up from the table abruptly and drink my glass of wine in one go. Clare looks at me in shock. I tell them that I need to check on something and depart the room.

I walk out to the garden and find Luke locking the garage.

He looks surprised to see me but still finds the time to admire himself in a glass panel. I unlock the garage and gently push Luke into it. I breathe heavily and smile as I think that if we were in a painting, it would be titled 'Two clichés in a garage'. I really despise being predictable but needs must.

I have an egg to fertilise.

I look Luke in the eyes and say 'Now'. He lifts me up.

A little while later, I walk back into the dining room, adjust my clothes, and sit back down opposite my in-laws. I am flushed and my clothes are slightly rumpled. Clare asks me if I am OK, that I look like I may be running a temperature.

"Isn't that right, Paul?".

Paul is too busy devouring a lamb shank and just nods politely. I reply that my meringues were giving me trouble. I am tempted to tell Clare that I was out in the garage getting pregnant, but I decide on second thoughts that maybe that would be impolite dinner party conversation. I offer her After Eights instead. My parents-in law watch me as they devour minty chocolates and cast the little paper cases away aggressively. I smile demurely at them. No-one can blame me, I think.

Life is all about eggs.

In the end

CHAPTER 3

MARTHA:

Mum always told me to try and banish my notions. I'm inclined to get carried away with them. Apparently. Granny used to say that my parents were too old to have me. She thought that they treated me like the Murano glass swan which she had brought back from Italy for me. I removed it from its box, carefully took the tissue from it, held it to the sunlight that streamed in from the front of the house and straight into the drawing room to illuminate the turquoise swan. I played with it for a few minutes, then asked Dad to put it on the top shelf of the bookcase where it remained for my childhood. Granny went to make tea - proper tea, strained and decanted into china cups with yellow flowers on them. Mum and Dad paused their recital for a moment to talk to Granny about Italy and her travels with her bridge club. I took my tea to the window seat and watched children on the beach below. Their muffled shouts reached me from my vantage point. I spent a lot of time on that window seat, framed behind glass, listening to my family with one ear. The other ear was tuned into the happenings on the beach, girls and boys eating thick sandwiches and

walking into the water with just their underwear on. Mum
and I swam when the beach emptied. She liked to feel that
she had solo ownership of that part of the ocean.

"Just you and me, Martha", she'd shout above the waves.
It's the only time she ever raised her voice as it was bad
for a singer's vocal cords, according to her manager. I
used to take advantage of the shouting and shout back
over the waves to her, occasionally waving at Dad, who
was just a tiny dot standing at the drawing room window,
smiling at us. Maybe that was a notion too, but Mum and I
blew him kisses and even if we just imagined it, we were
sure that he smiled back. We'd swim for a while, dry
quickly in the old hard swim towels and run back through
the gate where Dad would have Mum's gin and tonic
waiting. I was allowed a tonic water with ice and lemon,
and we would drink to our health. Dad never swam with us
as he had what Granny always described as a bad chest
from a childhood bout of pneumonia. Mum was the
strongest of the two of them, full of life with the salted scent
of the ocean on her, singing and drinking her gin and tonic
down in a few greedy gulps, while Dad watched her smile
and talk animatedly. Granny often said it was difficult to be
the child of such devoted lovers, but they never excluded
me, the product of their great love affair.

I do have a girl's devotion to finding romance for myself,
which is probably hard to believe when I wear my nurse's
uniform, starched, and buttoned up. Mum and Dad taught
me that love is the ultimate reward. I walk the nursing
home with my practical skills and my no-nonsense
approach but inside my heart is open to options. I'll prove
to Granny, long gone now and buried under an oak tree

beside Mum, that I'm not a turquoise glass swan, fragile and perfect, awaiting life to smash me into pieces.

I arrive at the canteen in work, a twelve-hour shift ahead of me. I talk to Martina, the canteen lady and she asks me how I am, as she knows about Mum's death a year ago. She touches me on the hand, her knuckles swollen from a life immersed in hot water and detergent. I assure her that I am fine and still working on getting Dad to sit at his piano twice a day to practise. The bookings stopped after Mum died, the duo sliced in half by cancer. I am working on finding a singer for Dad so he can tour again, but mostly it's an idea that is half-formed as he spends each day walking the beach or curled up in his armchair staring out to Lambay Island. He has taken to smoking cigars again when he'd given them up a long time ago. Mary, our housekeeper, who is prone to a bit of drama, thinks he's got a death wish, smoking cigars to ensure his lungs become as poisoned as Mum's did. His is a furious habit, whereas Mum always made such an unfashionable habit appear almost elegant, an ornate cigarette holder sent from China by a fan held in her hand while she smoked. The elegant smoking habit killed her in the end.

I banish the thoughts from my head and tie my hair back with a ribbon. I have Mum's hair, sea- bleached blonde, unruly and snaking down my back. People tell me it's beautiful, but I alternate between deciding to cut it all off and gazing in the mirror admiring my legacy from Mum. I take my tea and scone to a table where the rest of the staff sit. Tony races to pull a chair out for me. I take my place reluctantly beside him and greet my fellow nurses. Tony has a nervous energy that leads to the constant movement of at least one of his limbs. He invades my space, and I can smell the faint trace of alcohol from him. I appear to have an admirer.

I've taken to gazing at Conor. I try to watch him without drawing attention to it. Tony talks about his Saturday night out, 'bladdered, out of it, trying to shag someone down an alleyway'. He looks at me for admiration of his antics. I just smile and think he needs a new approach to romance. His seduction routine may need a bit of fine-tuning if it's me he wishes to win over. Although, I think that game may already be over. He lost me at 'trying to shag someone down an alleyway'.

Conor sits at a table with one of the Filipino orderlies. Occasionally, the two of them glance at Tony and his raucous crew as they slap backs and swap made up conquest stories, spitting bread and soup at each other in some bizarre male bonding ritual. I am aware that I spent five years at an all-girls' convent boarding school and struggle to adjust to my workplace, but even I'm not buying their attempts at worldliness. Conor reads a book and writes notes into a notebook. Tony leans back in his chair, revealing three inches of pale, hairy midriff, looks at me and then connects my gaze to Conor.

"The fucking state of your man. I'm not even bothering to study for that exam. You'd want to be thick to fail it", he says.

Some of his crew laugh with him, but most people at the table are uncomfortable and suddenly find their plates of food fascinating.

Conor looks over at our table, watches Tony briefly and then smiles at me. I wave back, in an awkward movement which is halfway between the Royal wave and that 'I'm slowing down' gesture which I learnt for my driving test.

"You're such a klutz", Dad would say if he saw me, in that fake New York accent he puts on to make me laugh from time to time.

Tony leans in close to me, the stale smell of lager fills my nostrils, and he says,

"Got the hots for Conor, then, Martha?".

"Mind your own business", I reply. He touches a loose strand of my hair and fixes it behind my ear.

Conor watches and rises from his seat abruptly.

I push Tony's hand away and leave the canteen following Conor and can hear Tony telling the rest of his crew,

"Tell you, she fucking loves me. She's gagging for it".

I follow Conor and see that he's stopped outside Room 12. He touches the door gently as I approach.

"Hi Conor, are you OK? You're studying for that Carer's exam?".

He still has his hand on the door and is startled as I speak. He turns around, just as the sun creeps down the corridor, illuminating his green eyes. I internally chastise myself for behaving like one of Jane Austen's quivering ladies. I am tempted to swoon.

"Oh yeah, hi, Martha…no, I'm fine. I'm just not one for studying, you know? I just prefer to keep moving, doing stuff".

"Well, I'm sure you'll do fine in the exam and…"

Conor realises that he still has his hand on the door and while I'm impersonating a patronising teacher with one of her struggling students, he interrupts and says,

"Yeah, sure. Look, I've got to go".

He walks away from me, leaving me to ponder over the mystery of room 12 and why I have learnt nothing in my twenty-two years to advance my romantic love-life.

Gerard, the home's manager, walks out of his office and greets Conor as he walks towards him. They laugh and chat easily as they stand by the Home's Mission Statement, which is framed in pride of place in the hallway. It hangs loose on the wall and Gerard stands purposefully beside it, a hammer in his hand.

"Conor, hold the corner of that for a second while I fix it", he says.

Conor holds it and reads the statement as they adjust it back on the wall.

"I've always thought that Mission Statement sounds like a Hollywood movie. With astronauts in it", he says to Gerard.

Gerard laughs and replies,

"We boldly go where no-one else wants to go".

They laugh and I feel excluded from their closeness, so I say goodbye in a voice so low they don't hear me.

I walk away, talk some sense into my love-struck head, summon up my nurse's patient smile and begin my rounds.

CHAPTER 4

ANGELA:

Matthew arrived back sometime during the night. He slept in the spare room, or I should say one of the spare rooms. I'd better get ready to be the good Angela, the perfect corporate wife – high- heeled stilettos, low cut tops, playing the game with ego flattering and gently adjusting Matthew's silk tie with soft hands, nail-varnished in this season's hot colour.

Oh, such a successful husband you are, darling, as he heads out to his glass surround office to be a tiger. Rarr, tiger! Go roar! To my shame, I've uttered the tiger roar over breakfast while buttering croissants and pouring freshly squeezed orange juice, flown in from an orange grove in Spain which uses no chemicals.

I spent most of the night after the tryst with Luke with my legs in the air, praying to be pregnant. Well, not praying exactly, doing deals with whoever runs this universe, angels, gods, devils, sprites. I'm not particular, as long as they get the job done. I'll worry about my soul some other day.

I shower for a long time. It's been two weeks since Luke and I just know he's hit the target. I dress in taupe and beige, spray Chanel liberally and join Matthew for croissants with a 'w'. He gets antsy if I pronounce the 'r'.

I fix his tie, ten points, trail my fingers down his chest, kiss him on the lips and pretend I'm inhaling his manly, successful scent. Fifty points are awarded to me.

"Gotta go, soon, Ange", he says, packing up his briefcase and collecting his costume of coat, designer sunglasses and his mobile phone which stops short of predicting the future.

"Catch you later, hon", I say, buttering French baked goods and for once planning to eat them. Eating for two. I smile and lean back in the pretending to be leather kitchen chair.

"You look happy?", Matthew says.

I notice the question in his voice and remind myself to keep up the sunshine and flowers Stepford housewife act.

He leans over and kisses me on the top of my head. He walks to the back door as Luke drives into the side passageway of the house with a van that needs its exhaust fixed.

I kiss Matthew goodbye and whisper,

"Sure, why wouldn't I be, darling?".

I remember the 'darling' at the last moment. He likes that, Matthew. He needs a lot of reassurance for a designer-clad tiger. Luke honks the horn and waves at us, mid embrace.

Matthew watches him taking tools from his van for a minute, turns to me and says,

"Watch your step with Bob the Builder. There's something about him I don't trust".

He leaves, admires Luke's tools in an exaggerated way. I smile thinking that the closest he gets to a work tool is when he cracks walnuts on Christmas Eve. I close the door, devour three croissants and text Lucy.

-all set, hon? Lunch on me, luv Ax-

-got my body-con dress on & return DART ticket in my dainty little hand. Magic fat reducing pants not working though, cu 1 pm, luv Lx-

I'm too cowardly to face Luke this morning, so I phone for a taxi to avoid walking out to the garage, where he is tearing down walls. Five minutes later, a taxi arrives out on the front drive. The taxi driver gets out and opens my door for me. It would appear to be a gentlemanly gesture, if I didn't know how much they value Matthew's account. I settle myself into the taxi and exit Tudor Drive.

'Tudor Drive offers an exclusive gated lifestyle for the affluent power couple. It is situated in coastal Dublin, a leafy suburb which prides itself on a chic village atmosphere with unrivalled views of Dublin Bay', the brochure promised. Matthew suggested to the estate agent, Elaine (blonde bob, camel coat) that the residents may sue if the brochure description was not adhered to. Elaine Blonde Bob looked fearful at the open day when

Matthew said this to her. She was handing us forensic crime scene white shoes and chain store champagne and you could almost see her brain working out how she was going to keep leaves on trees in Autumn/Winter.

Matthew and I laughed a lot then, back before ovulation kits and skittish financial markets.

We bought the house on the spot, Matthew only viewing the office and master bedroom.

"You had me at exclusive gated lifestyle, Elaine", he said, and we toasted our wonderful affluence there in the master bedroom while she muttered about putting our stamp on it. She fake giggled so much at Matthew's flirtation, that her champagne went down the wrong way and came out through her nose. She was a professional through and through and managed to keep the booking deposit cheque away from her body and free from sneezed, tepid champagne.

The taxi passes the dog walkers, the nannies with the latest in pram fashion and the ageing ladies with bejewelled fingers and disappointed eyes.

The driver talks to me, and I utter the occasional 'yes really' and 'shower of useless gobshites', as I'm assuming he's talking about the government again. I have this same conversation every time I get into the taxi with him and am fond of him in a small way. I do worry about the purple shade of the veins in his neck and how he's going to be able to pay for his eldest son, Wayne, to get to Oz next year, if the purple veins lead to fatal illness. The taxi driver talks about Oz like it is a wonderland and similar to the movie version. I am anxious for Wayne when he arrives there, wearing his Dublin jersey and spending his father's hard-earned money on a shared bed system, in a hot suburb in Sydney.

"You see, the thing about Oz is that it may be just a fairy-tale and the whole dream may just amount to a man hiding behind a curtain", I say out loud by mistake.

The taxi driver coughs politely and is briefly at a loss as to what to reply to me. He opens his window and says,

"Judy Garland had a tragic life, didn't she? I had a cousin who was the spit of her and Jesus, the state of her when she started drinking too much vodka...".

He's safely back to his monologue, so I take a deep breath, lean against the Febreze-sprayed leatherette seat, and watch the airplanes fly high over Howth Head. Fly safely, Wayne and find the Oz you want. I am conscious of a strange attachment to Wayne, place my hand on my taut stomach and spend the rest of the trip into Dublin conjuring up an image of a beautiful, new-born baby.

I open my eyes suddenly and remember to text Matthew.

-Can you get home early tonite? Missing you, Axxx-

Matthew's reply pings back straight away, he understands the Axxx code.

-I can be. Mx-

He's stingy with his typed kisses but seduction is a must if dates are to be kept feasible.

I reply with a string of 'x's and text Lucy.

-Pulling up outside Art Gallery. Are you there? -

She doesn't reply and I pay the driver and step into the spring sunshine.

I turn around and there she is. Lucy. Her blue eyes are bright, and she's dressed in her usual layers, a peaked hat with a flower corsage on it decorating her auburn hair. She walks towards me, talking as she does,

"Great, Ange, you saved me some credit there. Christ, the cost of it. Dave says I need to cut down on the texting. But Jesus, I'd go mad if I didn't have my mobile. Otherwise, I'd start to think of food. Look at the size of me and Jason's six months old.".

She places her hand on her generous middle region and continues,

"… and if I'm not texting, I have to find somewhere else to put my fingers and we both know where that'll lead, into a biscuit barrel and I'll get fat and have to enrol for Operation Transformation and stand in Lycra on national television, being weighed every week while everyone at home calls me a fat ugly cow with self-control issues".

I lean into Lucy, smell her usual scent of roses, and hug her, hoping some of her spirit transfers to me.

"Ange", she says,

"Black day, is it? C'mon, hon, let's look at art".

We link arms, me - taupe-robed and Lucy - a gypsy bundle of indigo and jade and walk together past the amused guard as we laugh together.

We walk towards the current exhibition and Lucy elbows me as a gathering of turtle-necked patrons walk quietly around the room. They pause at an expensive painting with squiggles of orange painted in the centre of the canvas and make suitably impressed noises. Lucy starts to laugh because the atmosphere is church-like. She gathers herself together and proceeds to admire the paintings with me.

"What would I do without you, Angela? I'd be ironing tracksuits in front of Jeremy Kyle if you didn't take me to places like this".

"How's Amy?", I ask her.

"She's grand, six going on sixteen. She's a handful, you know, Ange, full of madness and mischief'.

I admire a painting which consists of yellow stripes and reply,

"Tell her Aunty Ange is going to take her for a shopping spree soon, will you?".

"She'll love that. But don't go too mad, huh?", Lucy replies.

We both laugh as we remember the last shopping trip, a fashion-crazed Amy clutching so many bags that her fingers were sore for days after.

I hug Lucy and say,

"Keep her safe".

Lucy smiles with tears in her eyes and says,

"You know I will. We will".

We sit on a tiny bench and talk and laugh so much that a guard comes over to us and asks us to be quiet.

Lucy stands up and watches as a polo-necked lady buys the orange work of art.

She whispers into my ear,

"5,000 Euro for the baked bean picture. Jesus, Ange. I should get Amy to sell her school paintings, instead of using them to paper over the cracks in the paintwork".

I stand and laugh with her and the guard gestures for us to behave, so we walk briskly towards the coffee shop.

Lucy salivates as a woman brings trays of quiche through from the kitchen.

"Food I don't have to prepare doesn't count as calories, Ange, right? OK I'm having quiche and salad to be good and that massive chocolate tart".

She is so obsessed by the beautiful food that she doesn't notice that I clutch my stomach, the familiar stabs of pain blocking out my good mood and just as I think, no, not on my Lucy day, I know it's happening again.

I walk briskly towards the women's bathroom. Lucy is oblivious as she chats to the waitress about how much she is looking forward to eating the food. She turns briefly to talk to me, but I am in a corridor, walking towards the bathroom.

I find a free bathroom, confirm my fears, and check my handbag. I've been so convinced I'm pregnant that I haven't packed any Tampax. I sit on the toilet, head in my hands. I hear the noise of the restaurant reach me as someone enters the bathroom.

There's a knock on the door of my cubicle.

Lucy talks quietly.

"Ange? You in there?".

"Yeah", I say in a small voice.

"What's up?".

"The usual".

Lucy sighs and walks away, and I can hear coins being dropped into a merchandising unit. She slides a Tampax under the door. I sort myself out and join Lucy at the mirror as she brushes her hair, an anxious look on her face.

"Fuck it, Angela, it's so unfair", she says.

I fix my makeup and brush my hair. Lucy attempts to hug me, but I pat her on the shoulder and say,

"No sympathy, Lucy. It'll just kill me. Seriously".

We fix our faces like we have done so many times before. Lucy watches me re-assemble my flawless look and starts to laugh.

"It's not funny, Lucy", but I'm starting to laugh too, a slightly hysterical one but a laugh all the same. Lucy tries to talk, but snorts instead.

"But that guy, Luke? I thought myself that he would do the job. For fuck's sake. He must have been firing blanks".

I blink as I'm reminded of the image of Luke and I in the garage.

"Well, at the very least I hope you had some fun", Lucy of the silver lining philosophy, says.

'C'mon, we'll head home. You are not in the mood now, Angela. We can do lunch again some other time".

I steer her towards the restaurant queue, and she hesitates.

"Lucy, nothing is going to stop you having your lunch day. I insist".

She smiles at me and chooses lunch for both of us. Me and Lucy, united against the world, always.

CHAPTER 5

MARTHA:

When I arrive each morning, Martina in the canteen, has a scone ready for me. She waits till she sees me, slices it and pops it into the microwave. She pours me a mug of tea from the stainless-steel tea pot and brings it to me. I tell her that I don't need special service, but she just murmurs and says I need a bit of mothering.

On a Spring morning, I sit at a window in the canteen, enjoying a rare moment of silence. The last shift hasn't finished, and the new shift workers are arriving in dribs and drabs. I drink my builder's tea and smile as I think of what granny would make of me drinking out of a large, chipped mug with not a tea-leaf in sight. I feel a little happier this morning as Dad seems to have made a little progress. I found him at the piano yesterday evening, sipping black coffee and attempting to organise his music sheets.

"I can't sleep, you know, Martha", he said, his back to me as I watched him from the doorway. I walked into the room and placed my hand on his.

"I know, Daddy", I replied, the use of my childhood name for him bringing a tear to his eye.

"She should have told us that she didn't feel well. We could have done something sooner", he said.

I sighed and walked over to the window shutters, reaching to open them.

"She would have hated being a patient", I said as I pulled the shutters open.

"Martha, would you mind leaving them closed? I am not ready yet", he asked me.

I plunged the music room back into darkness, pressed some switches on table lamps and kissed him on the forehead.

I left him there in the dark room, pausing on the stairway as I thought that I heard a sound. And there it was, the first notes he's played since Mum died twelve months ago – the unmistakable opening notes of Beethoven's 'Moonlight Sonata'.

Progress, Martha, I thought, a smile forming on my lips.

I'm daydreaming as I finish my breakfast and watch the car park fill up with staff. I see Tony arrive, stretching as he locks his car door. He looks directly at me and blows a kiss. I become mobilized, deciding not to be trapped by his weekend stories of debauchery. I thank Martina and she smiles sadly at me. She's a good and kind lady, raising three kids with an absent father but tends to be attracted to dark dramatic stories. I tell her that I'll see her at lunchtime and collect my patients' notes from the front desk. I'm pleased to see that Peter is on my list today and walk briskly towards his room, greeting people as I walk. I pass one of the orderlies helping Mrs. Quinn to her chair-aerobics class. I pause and admire her outfit today, a lilac velour ankle length dress, which matches a knitted rose slide in her auburn tinted hair. The slide is slightly loose as

Mrs. Quinn's hair is reluctant to be tamed. But Mrs. Quinn is a former ballroom dancing queen and refuses to age in what's considered an age-appropriate way.

"Well, Martha, what do you think?", she asks me, a hand on her hip, as she attempts to stand straight, leaving just one hand on the walker, which makes her wobble slightly.

"I think you look amazing", I reply and can't help but notice that she has a pair of high-heeled patent leather shoes on. Her feet are crammed into them, looking painful and swollen.

The nurse assisting Mrs. Quinn smiles as she sees me look at the swollen feet and whispers into my ear,

"She refuses to wear old lady's shoes".

I laugh and think of the rows of navy, brown and grey orthopaedic shoes gathering dust in the back of Mrs. Quinn's wardrobe.

"Is that the lipstick I found for you, Mrs. Q?", I ask.

She pouts her lips and says,

"Yes. I love it, Martha. My grandson told me I looked awesome".

I smile as I walk away, glad that she loves the Elizabeth Arden 'Pink Violet' shade from the 1950s. I had scoured the internet for it and eventually found a full box of it belonging to a Mrs. Shirley Upton in Utah. Shirley had worn the shade all her life from when she had met her beloved Henry at a tea party on a lawn. We had a lengthy Skype discussion, facilitated by her daughter, Jan. Shirley had decided that she needed to get rid of the last box of the lipstick and try some new shades of lipstick before she 'enters the next realm' - her words.

Her daughter, Jan, informed me that Shirley had taken to wearing a Marilyn Monroe lush red shade on her lips.

I think of the two old ladies as I walk towards Peter's room and delight in the fact that they know the power of a well-turned-out pair of lips each morning.

I arrive at Peter's room, and I'm surprised to find that it is dark with no curtains pulled open. We are not supposed to have favourites here at 'The View' but I have to confess to a soft spot for Peter. They don't make gentlemen like him nowadays.

Peter has a heart problem. He's had surgery a few times and now just requires what's referred to as palliative care.

He has a talent for dramatization and tells us frequently that his ticker is about to stop any day now.

Today, his 'ticker' is fine, but Peter lies in the bed, immobile and with his eyes shut. I sit beside him at the bed, and he smiles when he feels the touch of my hand on his.

"Lady Martha. I'm not feeling too good today. I didn't sleep too well last night. Do you think you could find Conor? He's got a lovely voice for reading".

I blush slightly when he mentions Conor and Peter opens his eyes slightly and smiles at me.

"He's a lovely boy, Martha. You promise me you will take care of him. God, I love a bit of romance, makes the day go a bit faster".

"I'm not sure what you mean", I begin to say but even as I'm saying it I know it's a case of the lady do protest too much.

"Go on, bleep him on your pager yoke, Martha of the beautiful hair", Peter says, and I reach into my pocket and ask reception to find Conor.

Moments later, Conor arrives and knocks on the door.

"Come on in", Peter says, "we're all decent here".

Conor walks in, a well-thumbed book under his arms. He smiles as he greets me and Peter. I offer him my seat and tell him that Peter needs a nap as he slept badly last night.

"Thanks, Martha", he says as he sits down. My heart somersaults and I berate myself for my teenage type of behaviour and try to use up some energy to plump up cushions.

"It's an old book that he has. His mother left it in a box for him when she gave him up", Peter informs me. I look at the book, 'The Selfish Giant' by Oscar Wilde. Conor looks embarrassed and I ask him,

"I didn't know that your mother left you. That must have been…emmm…it's a lovely book and she must have loved you very much to buy something so beautiful for you".

Conor smiles a half-smile and starts to read from the book. I plump up the same cushions as I listen to the familiar words from my own childhood days.

"Every afternoon, as they were coming from school…"

Peter falls asleep as Conor reads. After a while, when he is sure Peter is sleeping, Conor closes the book. He stretches his black-denimed legs and says,

"Works every time", and he stands up and nods at me as he leaves the room. I tuck Peter in and sit in the chair that he's vacated and can smell his scent of nicotine and something citrus-like, lemon or lime.

I smile to myself as I think, oh you have it bad, Martha, sniffing chairs for lemon scent. But then again, it's good to feel something which takes me away from my home by the beach, windows closed to banish the sea air, forcing myself and Dad to survive amidst the trapped atmosphere of grief. Conor reminds me that a part of me still survives.

I leave Peter's room and continue my day. When Peter awakens, I remember that it's family visiting day. I help him get dressed.

"Suit please, Martha", he says, and I help him shave and brush his hair.

I reach into a locker drawer to find his Brylcreem as I know that Peter is a man who likes to point his best foot forward.

We face the mirror, Peter and I.

"Not bad, Martha, you remembered where to part my hair", he says, happier now that he's slept, a little bit of colour reaching his waxen cheeks.

"They used to queue up, you know, Martha".

"Who did?", I ask.

"In the ballrooms all over Dublin - blondes, brunettes, redheads. I wasn't the best looking of the boys, but I could dance and always had great hair".

I smile and reply,

"I can certainly see how that happened. Nearly finished now, Peter".

Peter admires his hair, somehow seeing a version of himself he likes in the mirror. I try hard to ignore the version I see, thin hair over a dry scalp, tiny tufts of hair clinging on like lichen. He says quietly,

"He'll come today. I can just feel it".

I know he is talking about his brother, Bernard, and instead of building false hope, I wheel him quietly to the resident's lounge, where the excitement of family visiting has spread to all the other residents.

I place Peter in his wheelchair by the window. Conor brings a cup and saucer to the table.

"Can you bring a second one for Bernard?", Peter asks him.

Conor smiles and fetches a second cup and saucer.

"He's not coming, is he?", I ask Conor as we leave Peter and help everyone else get settled.

"He never does", he replies.

We stand at the back of the lounge and watch as all the

families arrive. It's my favourite part of the week here. I'm not so fond of the latter part of the day, when the visitors leave, and the lounge is empty. I look and see that Peter is still sitting by the window. It grows dark in the lounge and the headlights of the cars outside make shadows all over the walls. Conor walks into the room and clears the cups from Peter's table, the tea cold and untouched in both cups.

He leans down to where Peter sits and talks to him quietly. He wheels him back past me and Peter says,

"Next week, Martha. He'll come next week".

I pat him on the shoulder and they leave the darkening room. I tidy up after the visitors, walk to the staff room and pack up my belongings from the locker and leave the home for the day.

As I walk towards my car, Tony and a group of my colleagues laugh and chat by his car.

Tony sees me and shouts across at me,

"Hey, Martha, we are heading for a few scoops. Are you up for it?".

I hesitate for a second, begin to say that I am not interested, but the thought of facing the shuttered house on the beach suddenly doesn't appeal to me and I say,

"Go on, sure why not?".

Tony has a cat that got the cream look and for once looks slightly nervous as he asks me if I want to travel in his car with him.

I am not sure that I want to be in such close proximity to him but decide to take the lift as I've never been to the pub they discuss all the time and feel the need for some fun.

"I'll be back in one second. I just need to get my coat from my car", I tell my colleagues and as I walk away, I hear Tony telling them that he's 'in'. I shudder slightly as I grab my coat. As I lock my car, I see Conor start his motorbike near to where I stand.

I walk to him and touch his shoulder. He startles but turns off the ignition and removes his helmet.

"Oh, hi, Martha, emm thanks for helping with Peter today. He's fast asleep now".

I interrupt him and talk too fast, afraid that if I stop, I will lose all courage,

"Conor, would you like to come for a drink? Just to unwind, have a laugh?".

He smiles and just when I think he is about to say yes, Tony beeps his car horn very loudly, walks around to his passenger door and shouts at the top of his voice across the car park,

"Your carriage awaits, my princess".

Conor starts to put on his helmet and says,

"I think I'll leave it. I kind of thought you just meant the two of us. You know, not for a date kind of thing, no, not that at all, but you know just …"

He runs out of words, puts on his helmet and I watch as he travels fast towards the gate lodge, where he lives at the edge of the grounds.

I don't notice that Tony has arrived until he speaks, very quietly, for him.

"Martha, you don't really have the hots for him, do you?".

I ignore what he says and ask him,

"Why does Conor have a house on the grounds, Tony?".

Tony hesitates, looks towards the group, gestures for them to go on and when they have departed, he takes my hand and walks me to the side of the building. He moves a rose bush with his hand and a stone cross can be seen, moss-covered and chipped. I kneel and look at the inscription, taking some tissue out of my bag to clean it.

"In memory of the children of St. Jude's", I read.

"What? There was an orphanage here? Tony? But Conor?".

I look towards where Conor's gate lodge is.

Tony sighs and says,

"Conor is the last of the Saint Jude's kids. They all got picked, but he was the last one left here".

I glance at the building and think of Saint Jude and all his hopeless cases who were once housed here. Tony takes my hand, and we leave to join the group at the pub. The sound of Conor's motorbike is long gone.

CHAPTER 6

MATTHEW:

I like to sit in my office on my own, a lot. I look out at the rooftops of Dublin and admire the building cranes. Ninety per cent of them are there because I put them there. No-one wants change. They would still have horses and carts, hoops for toys and children with rickets if it wasn't for people like me. I like to think I'm a visionary. I can look at a run-down piece of back lane property and see the possibilities. Hire an artist, paint a young urban couple on a brightly lit poster making dinner for their tax paying, safe game playing steady little friends. And bingo! The deposits come flying in. People have converted to aspiration like it's a new religion. The new commandments – envy everything your neighbour has – wife, car, holiday home in Spain, golf membership, kids in the right schools. Irish people have finally found a religion that gives them no guilt. So, sue me for giving them what they want. Our history has led to a national phobia of being at the mercy of landlords, so we sign twenty-five years of our lives away to a bank. Liberty is relative.

I've got a meeting scheduled in a few minutes. I've purchased a prime piece of land on the docks, full planning permission confirmed yesterday. It's not a good time to develop it, my accountant says, but I ignore ninety-nine per cent of what he says. He's a box ticking, number crunching, zero risk taking conservative. He can't see the future. Unlike me. I can hear sounds outside my office. I admire myself in the window reflection and take a deep breath, although it is not really required. I am on top of my game. Hennessy, O'Brien, and Walsh arrive at my office, talking animatedly. The sunlight highlights the bags under their eyes and illuminates their soft hands which have never had to dig a trench in the ground. Hennessy looks exhausted, which pleases me, as it gives me an advantage. He tends to be the hardest to convince, but he's acquired a new wife and he'll need more money. He shaves off a decade from each new wife's age every time he re-marries. Wife number three is in her early twenties – a gym bunny addicted to cosmetic surgery and her new prey's bank balance. She is a terrific actress, plays Hennessy so well that he doesn't notice minor things about her, like the fact that she hit on me at their society wedding last month. She sulked like a two-year-old when I turned her down. Angela is the only one for me, despite what the gossip columns say about me. If you are this successful, you are going to attract a lot of bloodsuckers.

I greet my three associates and we do the usual how's the wife/kids/enjoyed the rugby game, bullshit conversation. But it's compulsory. We need to remind ourselves why we do this, pretending it's for our families. Deep down, we know we do it because we can. Property development is like a narcotic fueled game of monopoly. Everyone wants to be Shrewsbury Road and if we end up with the cheaper properties, we will not be happy. Do not pass go unless you are in for the long haul. Hennessy starts the ball rolling by saying that he is over-extended. It's not like him to admit weakness. Wife number three is proving to be a demanding addition to his life. He writes a figure on a piece of paper and slides it across the desk to me and says,

"That's my max amount, Matthew. The banks are getting cautious. Take it or leave it!".

I take a quick look at the figure he's written down, smile, swivel in my ergonomic chair and turn away from them. I can hear Hennessy's slightly asthmatic breathing and say,

"You know, I have a lot of people interested in this deal. It's prime property with full planning permission granted and I have young professionals queuing up in estate agents' offices. Just waiting to own a well-appointed slice of West Wharf, a site that is currently full of rusting trailers and disused containers. It's going to be a prime site; I can feel it. I think you left your balls on the altar at your last wedding, Pat. I need two more million at least. I can find other investors".

I turn around, face him, and continue,

"Pat, you know, I want you in on this deal. We've been in since the beginning. When have I ever failed you?".

He pales and replies,

"Let me think about it, Matthew. I'll get back to you".

Walsh is one of those fleshy men who's never been in a gym in his life, wears shiny grey suits and has hairs sprouting from every facial orifice. He picks up a silver-framed photograph of Angela and me. It was taken at a Hunt Ball and in it, I'm wearing my Paris purchased suit and Angela is dressed in a red lace dress. Walsh places his thumb on Angela's image, leaving a slight trail of grease as he does. I lean back in my chair, grab a mini basketball, aim it over their heads and towards the net on the wall behind them. Swish, it goes in first time.

"You know your new wife, Pat? The gorgeous Sasha?",

I ask Hennessy. He colours slightly and interjects,

"Susannah. Yeah, what about her?".

"She told me that she is an interior designer. She'd love a new project, apparently. Wouldn't that be a great wedding gift for her? I'm sure we could organise for her to be the main designer for the new project. It would be good to keep a beautiful girl like her busy with fabric swatches and paint charts. You wouldn't want her bored and hanging around bars sipping champagne and waiting for you to get back from business trips?".

Pat's cheeks flush and he replies in a sullen voice,

"I'm not sure what you are trying to imply there, Matthew. Susannah's completely loyal to me. I think you might be a little bit jealous?".

He laughs a fake laugh and O'Brien and Walsh join in, lads in the locker room, forty years past their last rugby match. If only you knew, Hennessy, you'd be a tiny bit furious at how loyal she is. I put my hands up, laugh with them, and then say,

"I jest. Pat, you need to lighten up a bit. Listen, let's go through the paperwork and let me convince you guys of how fucking fantastic this site is and then lunch is on me".

Walsh brings the photograph closer to him and gazes lustily at Angela's image. I take the photograph from him and move it to the other side of the desk, reminding myself to ask my secretary to sanitise it after this meeting. I open the West Wharf file, sell my socks off and by the time we are having our first course in the French restaurant which is Hennessy's favourite (I always do my homework), I've secured a gentleman's agreement for ten mill. That leaves about five million to get from them but for today that's enough. We drink our last brandy at 8 pm, (well they do, I've stuck to water all day and I need to keep sharp around these guys) walk to the pavement outside, slap backs and arrange to meet up with them again in a few weeks, to finalise our commitment. We wave Hennessy off first in a taxi, wishing him well with his new wife and he smiles as he thinks of his new acquisition awaiting him at home, his double chin wobbling with anticipation, a cigar protruding from his lips.

"Lucky girl", I say to O'Brien and Walsh as they take the next taxi, and they make the usual locker room boy sounds as they start their journey back to their luxury pads. Their wives will be waiting with dinner on the table, kids bathed, piano-rehearsed and tranquility inducing mood pills firmly locked in cut glass bathroom cabinets. I walk through town, enjoying the air and decide to ring Angela. Her phone goes to voice mail, and I wonder where she is and what she is up to. I walk to my office and decide to leave for the day. Twelve hours seems too short for me, captain of industry that I am, but I'm feeling good about the meeting today and decide to depart. I drive past bus stops and DART stations, briefly catching the eyes of the clocker inners, the nine to fivers and turn rap music up to max volume feeling glad that I am who I am and never have to use public transport. My phone rings. I ignore the incoming call. Mum. She can wait.

I'm not in the mood for listening to her this evening. "Why are you not providing a grandchild for me, Matthew? Have you seen the latest Facebook photos of your brother?", bathing newborns or building a new water supply system with his own bare hands, in whatever third world country he has now decided to bring his greatness to. Mum needs a new hobby. I am her only one now. I drive into our development and feel the usual pride. There's not a sound here unless you count the occasional lawnmower or satisfying splash from a swimming pool. I park the car and notice the workman is still around. He avoids my eyes. Guilty secrets, I think. I know Angela wouldn't touch him with a bargepole but something about him irritates me. He's way too good looking to be a builder. I should have chosen the guy from Kerry with the turn in his eye. I kill this train of thought, because it's the way losers think, as if any woman would look at anyone else, when they have me. I walk to the kitchen, pour myself a beer and check my mails. Hennessy and O'Brien have come back with a provisional agreement to supply funds. Walsh is acting all coy. I'm positive that he's still got his communion money and is partial to reading the financial pages way too much, for my liking. I switch off my phone when I hear Angela arrive in a taxi. She walks into the kitchen, kisses me on the cheek and asks me about my day. I waltz her around the kitchen and tell her that I may have just pulled the deal off. She doesn't look too overjoyed, so I stop and say quietly,

"It's all good Angela. You'll be pregnant soon and we'll have all this to offer Junior". I smile but she remains still, looks around the kitchen and sighs. Two days later, I'm having a shave in my favourite Turkish barbers off Grafton Street. As aftershave balm is applied to my skin, I hear a familiar voice in the seat next to me. Walsh is right beside me, shouting down the phone at some underling. He finishes his call and notices me.

"Matthew! I didn't see you there. Great place, this? I haven't seen you here before. How are things?".

I smile as I say,

"Great. Yourself? Had any more thoughts about West Wharf?".

His smile fades and he gesture to the barber to finish. We sit with towels around our necks, facing each other. Walsh leans towards me and replies,

"You know, Matthew, how much I love working with you. But my partners are reluctant to get into this new one. They say a bad wind is blowing towards us".

I remove the towel from my neck and say,

"Come on, James. You're the boss. You're not telling me you've started listening to your accountants. There's a shit load of cash to be made from this development. You know that".

Walsh stands up, pops his phone into his jacket pocket and says,

"I know, Matthew. Look, leave it with me for a few days".

We both pay and walk onto the street.

"How's Angela?", Walsh asks.

I remember that he has been in the spare room for a while since his last dalliance with a former Irish model and touch him on the arm.

"Must be lonely for you, James, since your wife decided to punish you? Listen, why don't I get Angela to throw a little drinks party for us? Hennessy and O'Brien too? We need to get together and just chew the breeze, you know?".

Walsh bites at the fishing line, hesitates for a moment and says,

"Count me in. You know I always love seeing Angela. She's a great girl altogether".

"You know, she'll be thrilled to see you too. I know how fond she is of you".

I try to block out the phrase 'sleaze-bucket' from my head, the phrase Angela uses for him on a regular basis.

"Great. Listen, text me the details and I'll do my best to get there", he says as he turns away, waving his hand as he walks towards his office.

I wave at him, smile, and walk away.

If I was a Disney movie cartoon character, I would definitely be whistling right about now.

CHAPTER 7

ANNA:

There's a woman sitting opposite me - in her early fifties, I'd say, well put together if you like that kind of style; flowery dress and a pink cardigan with a big string of chunky, purple beads (which remind me of my mother's rosary beads) wrapped twice around her neck. The woman has beautiful nails, painted purple to match her beads, I'd say, and her hands are soft. I hide my own hands under my handbag. I've always hated them. They are the opposite of the woman's delicate hands, who looks like one of my mother's old bosses, the ladies who's houses she cleaned. Mam was a cheerful sort, the type of woman who everyone called 'salt of the earth'. If she was salt, I was pepper; spiky, spicy, and likely to bring tears to a lot of peoples' eyes. Mam was content in the flats. She never looked for more. Whereas me, I always wanted more. The woman smiles at me, and I look away as I can see it's fake. Two minutes ago, she was on the phone to someone and while pretending she was fine, tears rolled down her cheeks and onto her purple beads, turning two of them black. Her make up is a mess now, smudges of black mascara sit in a dark pool on her cheek. There'll be no tears for me today. A woman must have her standards.

"Anna O'Donnell?", a nurse calls. She's all prim and proper and wearing a cardigan that's seen too many cycles of a washing machine. She has smart girl's eyebrows; thick, bushy, and un-plucked. I daydream for a moment about being a smart girl and how my life might have been different if I hadn't been born in the concrete Saint Joan's council block within spitting distance of the Five Lamps.

"ANNA O'DONNELL?", the nurse repeats and I come to quickly, as I realise that she's calling my name. I've got so used to being called my other name in Spain that I've nearly forgotten who I am.

"Yes, I'm here", I say, and I smile at the young nurse.

My hands are shaking as I walk towards her.

"Great, can you follow me?", she says, and I have to say that she has a certain kindness about her, as she walks with me towards a door with a plaque on it -Doctor B. O'Rourke.

"Take a seat there, Anna? Is it OK if I call you Anna?", she asks, as I sit down on the hard plastic chair. The shaking has moved to my legs now and I cross and uncross them to stop the nerves. Be brave, Anna, I chastise myself. I'm surprised when the nurse takes a seat opposite me. I look around expecting to see a doctor arrive, but there is no sign of anyone else. The nurse shakes my hand and says,

"Anna. I'm Brenda O'Rourke. Oncology consultant. I'm so glad that you decided to come today. I'm sure you are in pain".

I smile but I know I'm imitating the nice flower-dressed lady from outside as I can feel a tear on my cheek. I try to speak but the young doctor who is one of the smart girls and probably does all the right things and ends up with a plaque on a door in a Dublin hospital with her name on it, talks again.

"Anna, try not to worry. I know that's easier said than done. We are going to run a few tests on you. See exactly what's happening. Yes?".

I nod, like one of those bulldogs Arthur used to have on the back ledge of his car, remove my ugly hands from under my handbag and place them in a pointless protective gesture, over my chest. I watch the ceiling as the doctor examines me. I can never get things right anymore. I wore my best dress today, a sunflower sundress that I have worn on many happy occasions sitting outside our apartment in Malaga with not a care in the world except to keep our sangria glasses topped up. Everyone else in the waiting room was wearing skirts or trousers so that when they have to strip off, it's only the top half they have exposed to the world. Even with a hospital gown on, I know that the world is getting a good look at my Marks and Spencer's sensible pants. It's probably just as well that Arthur isn't here. He is allergic to women's troubles. I count the stains on the ceiling as the doctor examines me.

"Does it hurt?", she says, her cold hands probing.

"No, not at all", I say, lying to myself and to her, when there really is no point anymore.

I discovered the lump the day Arthur left me. I was standing in my shower trying to come to terms with the fact that there was only half an hour in between him telling me he was leaving and when he closed the door on the way out. I wasn't concentrating on what I was doing and, in a moment, straight out of a nightmare, I felt it there - a sore, hard, lump. I ignored it for a week and invented ways of dressing and washing without paying it any attention, but it stayed there, and I had to face the music. I didn't know what to do or where to go, as all my Spanish pals are good time friends, only concerned with cocktail hour and who's shacked up with who. So, instead of hanging around and destroying the atmosphere at the parties with my little ailment, I decided to book a Ryanair flight home. It took two hours to pack twenty odd years of my Spanish life. Not much for a sixty-year-old woman. I didn't even phone Arthur. I just popped the apartment's keys through his and his new woman's villa door. I must be getting soft because I even wished him well on the note, even though he had the nerve to replace me with a woman twenty years younger than me. 'You can't hold onto your man', Lizzy's voice said in my head. It just popped in there after twenty-five years of absence. Well, I suppose Lizzy is allowed to nag me from wherever she is now, propped up on a cloud with red lipstick on and sipping a Power's whiskey.

Thank God, my flat is still in one piece. Well, more or less, considering that waster nephew of mine had been living in it for the past few years. He disappeared ten hours after I arrived back in Dublin. I suppose I gave him a fright arriving back suddenly and destroying his rent-free life. He nearly jumped out of his skin, when I tapped at the hall door, wearing my bright Spanish clothes; greens and blues which made me stand out on the grey concrete of the balcony - a kingfisher visiting magpies.

"Jesus, I didn't recognise you, Anna, it's been so long, like, years. Come in", he said, running his hands through his bleached hair and I replied,

"Don't mind if I do", pretending to be delighted to be invited into my own flat.

He peppered all his conversations with the word 'like' and after a while it made my head hurt just to be in the same room as him and I hadn't any energy to clean up the place, so he vanished before I could ask him for cash to fix it all up. I'm beyond all that now. Dirty sofas and nicotine-stained walls are the least of my worries and he was always a waste of space waiting for his next hit.

'Serves you right', Lizzy says, in my head now. She's taken up residence there, since I arrived back, and I look behind me every so often feeling shivers run down my spine and I expect to see her standing there. She's always young in my imaginings, is poor Lizzy, long before she lost her looks and all the booze and drugs overtook her. I'm prone to daydreaming lately and lose concentration when the young doctor is explaining things to me and only snap out of it when she asks,

"Anna, are you OK?".

I am embarrassed as I don't know what she was saying and reply,

"Yes, sorry, my mind is all over the place".

She has kind eyes, smiles, pats me on the shoulder and says,

"You can get dressed now and I'll send you down for a Mammogram".

I put on my dress while she writes notes in a file and curse myself again for wearing a stupid dress when I'm being examined all day. As I stand up from the examination table, my head gets dizzy, and I try to steady myself. The doctor notices and calls a nurse through to help me. The nurse links her arms through mine and talks to be in a motherly tone as we walk towards the X Ray department. I walk towards it with a heavy step and a nurse greets me at the X Ray department door and says,

"Come on through, love, we were expecting you".

I'm a goner, now, I think. Once they start calling you love, you may as well get your last perm done, Anna, my old dear. I space out in my head for a long time and although they were so kind to me at the hospital unit, nothing went in and it's only when I'm in the taxi on the way home that I try out the new word.

"Are you alright, luv?", the taxi driver asks as we travel down the Malahide Road towards the North Strand.

"I've got cancer", I say, and the word makes my lips stick together. My heart races so much that I think I might just keel over here in the taxi and not even make it to the chemotherapy sessions, which the country nurse sorted out for me in such a chirpy voice that you would think she was organising spa treatments for me.

"Jesus Christ!", the taxi driver says and meets my eyes in the mirror. He turns up the radio, show bands – lovely. I must be in the only taxi in Dublin with a silent driver. Cancer, I say again in my head and place my hand gently on my treacherous left breast. Shame about your cleavage, Anna, you vain old cow. Joe Dolan sings up a storm in the car as we arrive at my flat and I think a little sadly that even Joe can't save this day. I pay the taxi driver and shuffle around for coins for a tip in my over-sized handbag, but he can't get away quick enough, like I'm contagious. I decide to spend the coins on something nice to cheer myself up in Mrs. O'Reilly's little makeshift shop on the ground floor of the block. Christ, I think, this place is even a worse kip than it was two decades ago, littered with beer cans and crisp packets. There is a knot of boys hanging around, watching my handbag. Some things never change. Different decade - same grey, hungry looking faces. I walk past them, and they snigger saying something about the state of my sundress. I hold my head high and walk into the shop where Mrs. O'Reilly still presides over and wait for her to say -Look what the wind's blown in-, when she pops her head up from where she was restocking crisps, looks me in the eye and says,

"Well, look what the wind's blown in. Anna, the bad penny, has turned up again. Thought you were in Spain with your fancy man?".

She fixes her cardigan, which I'm sure is the same one she was wearing when I used to live here, navy like a nun's. She's always had that nun's look about her, which survived intact even after giving birth to seven children.

"Howya, Mrs. O'Reilly. You are looking emm...neat. How are all your kids"?

She sniffs the air and says,

"Three in the 'Joy, last time I looked, but the others are grand. Got out of here and live in lovely houses, some of which have en-suites, I'll have you know. But now, what are you doing here? I thought with all the trouble before you'd never come near this place again. Why are you".

I cut in quickly as I hate her knowing my business.

"Just came back to catch up with a few of my old pals, you know. It gets very hot in Spain this time of the year, so I thought I'd take a little trip home to see what rain looks like".

We both look out at the rain cascading down the balconies to the car park below. She sniffs again and opens her mouth to interrogate me. I interrupt her before she can begin and say,

"Twenty silk cut purple, Mrs. O, if you don't mind".

She stands with her hands on her hips and looks right into my eyes. She's buying none of my bullshit story, so I walk away and leaf through the Evening Herald while she fetches the cigs. She almost throws them across the counter at me. I pay her and she says,

"They'll give you cancer".

I leave the shop quickly, not a bit surprised with my lukewarm welcome home. I light up a cigarette on the balcony and look straight over at Lizzy's old flat. Strangely enough, it looks well taken care of. It's got the only window box in the entire block with pink flowers growing from it. While I'm thinking that Lizzy would love that, I don't notice a young woman approach me. She's well-dressed for around here, wearing jeans and a khaki parka and has pretty hair tied up in a high ponytail. She walks towards me, and she waves at an older lady standing at a door just down from mine.

"See you next week", she says breezily, and the older lady blows her a kiss. She is still smiling when she spots me leaning over the balcony, enjoying a second cig (might as well be hung for a sheep as for a lamb) but her smile disappears once she clocks me and remembers who I am. She walks towards me so fast I haven't got time to get away and into my flat.

"You absolute bitch", she says, her cheeks flushed red and her eyes manic. "What the hell are you doing back here? Don't think anyone is going to want to have anything to do with you, Anna. You selfish bitch".

I back away from her a few steps but am wobbly from the hospital and not fast enough to get clear away. She raises her hand towards me, and I close my eyes as I wait for her fist to connect to my cheek.

"She's not worth it, Lucy", a voice says quietly. I open my eyes and see that her mother, Rose, has stopped her from hitting me. I feel a little saddened because Rose used to be a good friend of mine, a long time ago. They walk away from me briskly. I stand up straight, put the cigarette out and ask,

"How is she? How is ….".

The two women stop walking. Lucy turns around and walks towards me, angrily.

"Don't you dare! Don't even let me hear her name coming from your lips".

I bow my head in shame. Lucy's mother guides her back to her flat.

"Come on, love, a nice cup of tea will calm you down. You can't get into your car in that state".

Lucy is crying. I can hear her sobbing from here. I light another cigarette and look over at Lizzy's. I put my key in the lock of my door and as I'm doing it, a voice goes around my head and I'm not sure if it's mine or Lizzy's,

"You've got to sort it all out, Anna".

I shiver and shuffle into my flat, the exhaustion of the day sucking the last bit of energy from me so I can barely walk. I catch my reflection in the hall mirror as I walk past and don't much like what I see. Dead woman walking.

CHAPTER 8

ANGELA:

Luke is after another tryst. He hung around the kitchen a lot today with a hangdog look. I could almost feel sorry for him if I didn't hear his constant phone calls all day, arranging hook-ups with girls with Californian names – Trudi, Rochelle, Barb. He's barking up the wrong tree here. He and I were a one act play and the curtain has been closed there. I've taken my bow and I'll file that experience for the moment – unless Matthew has meetings around ovulation dates. He tells me I'm obsessed. About having a baby. I know he's not keen, but I'll be the one doing all the work, anyway. He knows that and he'll be free to fill Dublin full of lucrative buildings. I wonder why he needs so much money. We have too much anyway, more than I could have ever dreamt of. It's not about the money, he says. It's all about power and the thrill of the chase. The working on something for months and then watching it grow out of nothing. A bit like having a baby, so, I said to him. He gave me a withering look, but I'm growing used to those looks now. We used to be on the same page, Angela and

Matthew, Dublin's hottest couple, the life and soul of every party in Leafyville. Something's changing in me. I'm tired of the act. The perfect wife. The perfect house. The perfect parties. The perfect social life. It used to be enough. Not anymore. I'd swap it all for a baby swaddled in a blanket. Maybe I am obsessed. Or just lonely. Little orphan Angela, rescued by a tall, dark, handsome stranger and trapped in a beautiful box tied with a suffocating bow.

I close the blinds in the kitchen so I can no longer see Luke. If I'm honest, he was a nice diversion. Matthew is never around much anymore and if he is, he's on the phone the whole time, chewing food I've spent hours preparing, in minutes. I think I'll give up cooking. It's a waste of time and I only pretend to eat it as I must fit into the designer dresses I get delivered each month. It's exhausting, all this striving to be something I 'm not. But I'll hang in there until a baby turns up. Then, Matthew and I will be back as a team, not the hostile almost enemies we are at the moment. There's a lot of talk on the radio about the banks slowing down their lending and a market crash looming. I look around our lavish five bed, re-decorated every two years house and wonder if I would really care if it all disappeared overnight. Some days I think not but feel disloyal to Matthew for even having that thought. I walk to the drawing room, light candles, and check my reflection in the Art Deco mirror. I look OK - hair coloured dark, make up perfect, eyes tired but their vivid green colour accentuated by expensive make up.

I hear Matthew's car pulling up and adjust my cerise silk dress until it's just right. I've worn my highest strappy sandals, so I'm about the same height as Matthew. It's amazing what a couple of inches manages to achieve for a woman's negotiating skills. He walks towards me, and I hand him a glass of Cabernet Sauvignon. He's talking on the phone but finds a second to kiss me on the cheek.

"What's that? Oh, that was me just kissing Angela. I know! I am a lucky bastard. Yes, I will tell her you said hello", he says and ends his call.

"Thanks, Angela, that is just what I needed. You are looking good. New dress?".

I smile, lean in close to him and reply,

"New stock in today in Arabelle's. You know she likes me to have first pick".

Matthew touches the soft material and laughs,

"You haven't lost it, you know, Angela. Still as beautiful as you were in the foyer of The Phoenix Hotel all those years ago".

He's after something. We never mention where we met to people, we tend to just gloss over it with a made-up story of cocktails and love at first sight. I have spent the past twenty years trying to blank out the image of the old Angela. She's just a ghost now, an unwelcome image in our decadent French drawing room.

"Matthew, let's sit down by the fire. You know talk, have a conversation".

He checks his phone and looks hesitant to spend time with me. It rings and I say,

"Just switch it off. Please. For once".

He is sending a text back to someone. I wait patiently until he's finished, reach over, turn his phone off and place it in a Waterford Crystal bowl on the mantelpiece.

"Ah, Angela, I wasn't finished", he protests.

I take my own phone from my handbag, switch it off and place it beside his in the bowl and utter the phrase which most husbands dread,

"Matthew, we need to talk".

His face is unreadable as he joins me on the sofa He sighs as he sits down reluctantly and then he rapidly resumes his poker face, the façade that he has used in every business deal in Dublin.

"OK, what's up?".

He places his hand on my stomach and raises his eyebrows.

"No, I'm not pregnant. Actually, we need to have that conversation again", I say,

Matthew's face reddens slightly, and he stands up and commences to pace the room.

"We've got to face up to reality here. I've made some enquiries and have booked a provisional appointment for both of us at a fertility clinic. The best one in Dublin. They have an excellent success rate and their clients have written great testimonials".

I am conscious that I am presenting it like a business proposal and the more I do that, the more likely Matthew will attend. He fishes his phone out of the crystal bowl and switches it back on, sits back on the couch and remarks,

"That snake Walsh will not commit on this new project. I'm going to have to push hard on this".

He is distracted so I say,

"Matthew, did you hear anything I said? About the clinic?".

Good girl, Angela, keep it non-specific and he'll forget about sperm counts and sealed jars in labs being tested.

"Christ, Angela, I haven't got time for this. Just give it a few months. You'll get pregnant eventually".

I can feel my temper rising and say,

"For fuck's sake, Matthew, it's been five years since we started trying. If you turned up occasionally when I'm ovulating, I might have a chance".

He gets angry too and we'd been doing so well, the nicely dressed couple in the exquisite French room and say,

"You are getting boring, Angela. I'm not some kind of performing seal and I'm sick to death of all those sticks that you pee on, dominating my life. You can't just expect me to drop everything every time your stick says we should. It's just..."

I interrupt him there, sensing an end to my fertility clinic dream, so I change tack, walk over to him, sit on his lap and reassure him,

"Matthew, I'm sorry, sweetheart. It's just that I'm going to be forty later this year. I want a baby. I need a baby".

He relaxes a little and then checks his phone.

"Walsh is only going to come up with half the money. Jesus".

I sense an opportunity here, stand up and walk to the fireplace and light some mood-altering candles with names like tranquility and balm. I'd need a church full of them here tonight.

Matthew watches me and smiles.

"I'm sorry, Angela. My mind is all over the place. Look, if I get Walsh sorted, I'll have more time to concentrate on this baby thing".

I bristle at the 'baby thing' and pour us both another glass of wine. Matthew drinks half the glass in one gulp and says quietly,

"Ange, you know what we did in the earlier years. To persuade clients. You couldn't just bring that act back for one evening? I can have the guys around and if you work your magic on Walsh, I'm sure I could twist his fat little arm to part with the cash I need?".

There is a dead silence in the room and the tranquility fragrance doesn't appear to be effective as my heart is racing.

"I'm not sure I can go back to doing that. And with Walsh? I'd need to keep my eyes firmly closed".

I gag slightly as I recall Walsh's meaty hands and the feeling of nausea I experience every time he touches me. Matthew brightens as he knows I haven't ruled the idea out completely. He stands up and walks over to me at the fireplace, placing his hand on my hip. We are the same height. As he looks directly at me, I wonder how I can feel so attracted to this man who is offering me to a business associate for a development deal and say,

"If we sort Walsh out, can I go ahead and book the clinic appointment?".

He sighs, but I'm on a roll here and I fetch my own phone.

"When are you planning to have this drinks evening for your associates?", I ask.

He livens up a bit and finds his diary on his phone,

"This Friday? Get it out of the way?".

"Yes, OK. But before I enter that into my diary, can I just send a confirmation text to the clinic and say we'll be there on the 20th?".

I pretend I'm engrossed in my phone as I don't want to look at him.

"Yeah, go for it", he replies, and I ignore the reluctance.

I send the confirmation text to the clinic and forward it to Matthew.

He texts his colleagues and I listen to the ping of the replies, before returning to the couch.

Matthew sits opposite me, watches the candles flickering

and then leans over to clink glasses with me.

I pull myself together and toast him back.

"To us, darling", he says.

"To us, Matthew", I reply.

In my mind I'm moving a virtual Queen on a chessboard.
Moving her into position to claim the game.

"Checkmate", I say so softly that Matthew doesn't quite
hear me.

CHAPTER 9

MARTHA:

I've no need for Martina's motherly concern this morning. Or her scones. I breakfasted early with Dad. The two of us sat in the summer house and had a picnic breakfast of brown bread, blackcurrant jam and a cafetière of coffee. Dad was wandering the house when I woke, so with a heavy heart, I put together a picnic basket to take to the end of the garden. He ate nothing, but it got him out of the house for half an hour and he watched the ferries slide across the horizon. I accept a mug of tea from Martina as I'm too early for my shift. I face outwards towards the garden, where some of the residents are out tending to plants. Some are wheeled amongst the plants set into railway sleepers and they are hard at work pruning and snipping. They laugh and joke with each other as they work their gardening magic. Each snip with secateurs asserts their hold on this life and I admire their resistance to sitting tranquilized in high backed chairs while daytime television blares from the day room. Gerard runs a tight ship here and tries to give added value to the clients, in his words. He did a quick bit of research one day and set all the lounge area televisions to children's' channels. After three hours, he realised that no-one took any notice of what they were watching. This prompted him to set up a more rigid extra-curricular schedule – gardening, chair-aerobics, baking, art classes. I admire his attempts to respect the elderly, especially when it costs more money to provide these services, but the residents' children do require a lot of value for the astronomical fees each month.

I sit watching the gardeners and feel a bit of peace wash over me. Dad has refused all tours for another year. He spoke to his agent, who gently suggested that he may try and find a replacement singer for Mum, so that he can tour again. Dad took it badly and as I pointed out to him later that day, after he'd cut the agent off mid-phone call, he didn't suggest a replacement wife, just a singer. Dad is having none of it, so now his days stretch endlessly in front of him. I have an idea which may keep him busy. Granny's mews could do with a lick of paint and some refurbishment. A bit of physical activity will do him good, give him a sense of purpose and may remove some of the greyness from his complexion and mood. I write 'paint tester pots' and 'flooring' in my notebook and put it away to discuss later with him. I hear the staff arriving and the familiar voice of Tony amongst the chatter. I will try and avoid him today. I managed to escape him in the pub after work the other day, but I'm afraid that my acceptance of his invitation to go to the pub and my subsequent arrival with him will give him encouragement to hunt me down. He is confusing love with acquisition, as I am probably the only female staff member who hasn't had the dubious pleasure of joining him in his bed. It's all about him, this chase, this refusal to back down and accept that I'm just not interested in him. I am irrelevant, just a deer that constantly wanders from his hunter's sights.

There is some noise behind me, and I turn around to see what is happening. Conor is carrying a bundle of stuff. He places it on one of the tables and leaves the room again. I bring my tea to the table and sit waiting until he returns. Tony and his merry crew arrive. I greet them and smile but turn away avoiding further conversation. Conor walks past them, and Tony attempts his usual sadistic banter with him. Conor is oblivious and walks to the table where I sit. He wears black as usual and I notice his hair is newly cropped, almost soldier-like. His eyes are dark green, that colour which the sea becomes on November days. I shake myself to cancel my immersion into a full-blown daydream where I become a Daphne de Maurier heroine, on a high cliff in a corseted gown, hair escaping from its rigid bun, awaiting my man's return from sea. I am delusional.

Conor smiles at me and sits down next to me. He is shy and asks,

"Would you like to help me, Martha?".

My inner Daphne de Maurier character swoons slightly at the sound of my name being uttered by him. I ignore my thoughts and reply,

"Course I can. Who owns all this stuff?"

He looks sad and says,

"Mrs. Casey? She died during the night, and I guess I have the job of sorting through her things".

He puts a large cardboard box down on the table and turns it towards us.

No known relatives is written on it in large black letters. I remember Mrs. Casey for a moment and wonder how such a vibrant lady, who liked to sing and sew all day has been left with no-one to in her life to complete this task. Conor reads my mind and says quietly,

"Her husband died in a car crash when he was thirty. She had been a widow for...".

He picks up a file and reads her date of birth,

"...fifty-three years. They never had a chance to have

children, she told me".

I pick up some faded letters and read out loud a few phrases from them,

Meet me at the dance, my love. I cannot wait until you become my wife. All my love, always.

I feel like I'm being intrusive, so I fold them neatly and put them back on the table. Conor smiles at me and says,

"She said that her husband was only romantic when he had a pen in his hand and even when they were married, he left letters for her to find all over the house".

I place my hand on my heart and reply,

"That is so romantic. Oh, for one such letter. The most we girls can hope for nowadays is a text with 'luv ya' and some 'x's at the end.".

Conor laughs and opens an untidy basket of Mrs. Casey's embroidery.

"She liked her kittens", I remark.

"She couldn't bring any of her cats when she came here, so she thought she'd make some of her own", he replies.

We tidy them and spend some time cutting frayed edges and admire her handiwork of kittens in amusing poses. One of the pieces is almost finished. I trace the stitches and imagine Mrs. Casey going to her eternal rest sewing the stitches on the Easter kitten piece.

"I think I'll finish it for her, Conor? Do you think that would be OK? It seems a shame it's not finished", I ask.

"Can you sew?", he replies. He is busy sorting all the other possessions into neat piles – perfume bottles and trinkets, photographs of Mrs. Casey and her long-lost husband looking young and optimistic, books, pill bottles and the pretty embroidered cats.

"I learnt to sew in primary school. Sure, I could give it a go, it would be nice to challenge myself and finish it for her?".

He smiles and says,

"There is a box up on the counter beside Martina. It's got 'charity' written on it. If you go and get that, we can sort through the piles and then if anyone wants anything, we can ask them to donate some cash to the charity".

I walk up to the counter and take the box. As I'm returning, Tony stops in my path.

"Hey, Martha, it was great to have a date with you the other night. Fancy another one some time? Just you and me, on our own next time, maybe?", he asks.

I can see Conor watching and say,

"Sorry, Tony, I think you may be getting the wrong end of the stick here. I'd be happy for us to be friends, but that's about it. I'm sorry".

He is not impressed. His blue eyes narrow and become mean. He stretches his arms, a tactic he uses the whole time to display the results of his hours in the gym and says in a spiteful tone.

"What's your man got that I don't have? He's a bit of a weirdo if you ask me. Lives in that house out in the woods all on his own. Something not quite right in his head".

I walk past him and say quietly,

"I wasn't asking you, Tony. Just mind your own business".

He starts to speak again but I just walk away from him and join Conor at the table. Conor says nothing about Tony, although it is difficult to ignore his glare from the table opposite and his loud, braying voice. As we sort through the items, some for recycling, some for the charity shops, nurses and the occasional doctor arrive and take some items and drop money into the charity box. The nurses swoon over the love letters and I feel sad when they end up in a recycling pile. Conor puts the photographs in that box too but removes one wedding photo of Mrs. Casey and her husband, takes some coins from his pocket, and enters the money into the box. One of the doctors takes some of Mrs. Casey's old pill boxes and her trinkets are all ready to be despatched to the charity shop. I have a notion to send her love letters off in style, so I remove the red velvet ribbon from my hair and wrap it around them all, tying them prettily with the ribbon. Conor looks at my unruly mane of hair now that it has escaped from its usual prim nurse's bun, touches the ends of it where it curls and says,

"You have beautiful hair".

Tony walks up beside us as Conor touches my hair and laughs,

"Getting very cosy, you two, huh? Jesus, Conor, you're her latest lame duck, I'd say. She has a habit of doing that. Mother Teresa, she is".

He runs his fingers though my hair. I push his hand away and stand up to get away from him. Conor becomes withdrawn and starts to pack up all the items on the table. A porter arrives, takes all the boxes away and places the charity box back beside Martina. Tony laughs as Conor stands up and starts to walk away. He puts a hand on one of Conor's shoulders and says,

"I don't know what your game is, Conor. But I'm not fucking buying it".

Conor takes Tony's hand away from his shoulder and says quietly to him.

"Tony, I just want a quiet life. I just want to do my job and then go home. I don't want any trouble".

Tony gets aggressive and pushes him hard. Conor doesn't react and tries to walk away. Tony starts to lean in for a punch, but as he does, Gerard walks through the door, takes one look at Tony's purple face, points his finger at him and says,

"I told you before, Tony. One more complaint from anyone and you're out of here. Have you got a complaint, Conor?".

Conor says,

"No, I'm fine", and walks briskly away from the scene, avoiding all the eavesdroppers as he leaves the room.

Tony laughs and puts his hands in the air in surrender and says,

"Jesus, Gerard, me and Conor were just fooling around. Christ, can we not just have a bit of fun now and then?".

Fortunately for Tony, Gerard's mobile rings and he walks away, engrossed in his phone call. I am left at the table on my own as Tony re-joins his friends, muttering 'for fuck's sake' and notice that when Tony pushed Conor, his photograph of Mrs. Casey's wedding slipped from his pocket. I decide to bring it to him.

I leave the building by the back entrance. It's far away from the picture-perfect front of the building, where brass gleams, window baskets hang and the more lucid residents sit in the front lounge, just off reception - well-presented and playing chess. At the back of the building is where the kitchens and work rooms are found, a maze of laundry, bedpans and large bins with hazard warnings printed on them, for the discarding of needles and medical supplies. It's a busy place here, quietly industrious staff dealing with the grisly side of the home. I push open the back door and feel grateful to be outside away from the disinfected air. Conor walks ahead of me. I call his name, but he is not answering me. I take a turn to the left and find myself bending low to avoid the scratch of brambles. This path leads to a wood and once you are a few minutes down it, it becomes Little Red Riding Hood like in its density. I walk briskly to try and catch Conor. As I get further down the path and away from the noise of the home, I can hear the tinny sound of music ahead of me and I can see that Conor is wearing his earbuds. I walk faster, become careless, forget I'm bare-legged and scratch my leg on a bramble. I cry out, tell myself to stop being so babyish and Conor turns around and sees me attempting to clean the scratch with a tissue. I sit on the path to try and rest my sore leg and become aware of Conor standing over me. He sits down beside me, removes his earbuds, and says,

"Nurse, heal thyself".

I laugh and reply,

"You think I'd know better. Stupid brambles. I can see why the staff dare each other to come out here at night. It has a touch of the Neil Gaiman about it".

I point to the old graveyard beside us, which has various levels of stooped headstones, covered in lichen, and inscribed with the names of old nuns who lived in the convent before the home's time. The headstones are hard to decipher, and I walk towards them, leaning on Conor, although my leg is perfectly fine. Feminine wiles are a woman's prerogative.

"Sister Agnes. Lived her life with fortitude. God, that sounds like it was fun. Gathered in Jesus's arms in 19 fifty something. I can't read it. And look at all these little white crosses. There are so many of them. Thomas Burke. Oh shit, two days old. Patricia Murray, eighteen months old. Gone to her eternal rest. Do you think these are the babies from the orphanage, Conor?".

Conor has moved to the second row of the children's plot. He is cleaning one of the white crosses and is lost in thought. I walk up to him and gently place my arm on his shoulder. He jumps slightly at my touch, and I fill the silence with a babble of senseless chatter,

"God, I'm sorry, Conor, for giving you a fright. This place is giving me the creeps as well. Are you OK? You look like you've seen a ghost? Stupid thing to say. I was just following you. Now I sound like a stalker! Shut up Martha. I

86

was trying to find you because you left your photograph of Mrs. Casey behind when you left the canteen".

Conor snaps out of his reverie and smiles a small smile,

"Oh yeah, thanks".

He looks at my leg and continues,

"That looks sore. My house is just a minute or two from here. Would you like to come in and I'll find something for you to fix it. That's if you want to. You may just prefer to go back to the home".

I smile as I reply,

"I'd love to see your place. If that's OK? Like, you haven't got a secret wife locked in the attic or something?".

Conor replies,

"Is that what they say about me? In the canteen? That I've got secret wives locked up in my house?".

I walk closer to the cross he was cleaning, see that it says,

'Francis Doyle b. Jan 3rd, 1984'. I say to him,

"Conor, ignore me. When I'm feeling awkward, I tend to keep talking, to fill the silence kind of thing. Look, they say a lot of stuff about a lot of people in that canteen. I ignore ninety-nine point nine per cent of it. Boredom tends to breed gossip. Come on, I'm dying to see your house and your locked-up harem of wives".

We both laugh and start to walk along the path out of the graveyard. Conor looks back for a second at the grave of baby Francis and I say,

"Poor kid. They didn't even write down the date of his death. I'm so glad times have moved on".

Conor looks like he is about to say something but keeps walking ahead of me. I remind myself to keep my stupid babble to myself and we continue our Hansel and Gretel walk along the path until we come to a clearing and arrive out to the light. The gate lodge is like an illustration from a childhood book. It is made from stone and its window frames and front door are painted a teal colour. The front garden is planted with old fashioned tea roses and other bright coloured flowering plants and if I had paid attention to my avid gardening grandmother, I would know the names of them. Conor opens the wooden gate leading into the cottage and I brush past him to walk to the door. I inhale that familiar citrus scent from him and suddenly remember my manners,

"This is so beautiful, Conor. I've only seen it while driving past before but it is gorgeous close up.".

He opens the door and gestures for me to walk in. I walk past him and see that we are in the kitchen, which is sparse but clean. Conor fetches a first aid box from a cupboard and says,

"OK, Martha. You're a nurse. Would you like to clean the cut yourself? Or will I do it?".

I look at the wound on my leg, noticing for the first time that's its bleeding and decide to let him tend to me. He takes off his jacket, gets some water from the tap and tends to my wound. I notice that he looks after himself, as the muscles on his arm are taut. I pull my stomach muscles in as we stand there in silence in a moment of vanity and laugh. I remind myself to find a boyfriend or at least get out more if I'm imagining a work colleague wiping blood from a cut on my leg is stage one in a seductive ritual.

"What's so funny?", Conor says, a smile on his face as he puts a plaster on the cleaned wound. I inspect my leg and say,

"Oh, nothing much. I was just thinking how calm and normal your home is. No crazy women in the attic at all. They'll be very disappointed back in the canteen".

Conor packs away the first-aid kit and fills the kettle. I remove the photograph which he dropped in the canteen from my pocket and hand it to him.

"Thanks for sorting me out, Conor. Here's the photo you dropped. They were a very handsome couple. Poor Mrs Casey".

He takes the photograph from me and places it on the counter and hands me a cup of coffee. I drink from it and he leans against the kitchen counter, watching me.

"Do you have a boyfriend, Martha?".

I feel my cheeks flush and say what I say all the time,

"Me. No. I haven't time. But I live in hope. And you? Any woman in your life?".

Conor walks towards the door that must lead into the sitting room and replies,

"Emm…No".

I notice there are some female touches to the kitchen; a fabric heart with 'home sweet home' written on it and some photos of Conor with a blonde-haired happy looking girl pinned to a cork noticeboard.

"She looks nice", I say, facing away from him as I experience a minor stab of jealousy. Conor opens the door to the sitting room and casually says,

"Oh, yeah, that's Chloe. She worked here for a while, to earn some cash while touring Europe. She's back in the States now. She left about two months ago".

I lie through my teeth as I reply to him,

"You look good together. It's a shame she had to go home".

He replies,

"Well, she didn't really have to go. It's just that I am not too good at being with people after a while. I guess Tony may be right. I probably am a bit of a loner. I tend to be too quiet for most people". I don't reply as he is standing so close to me that I can see the tattoo on his upper arm clearly -veritatem voluntas ex. I pluck up some courage, touch his arm and ask,

"What is that Conor? Latin? Do you mind me asking you what it means?".

He touches my hand which is resting on the tattoo and says,

"You know, Martha. I'm probably not worth the trouble. I tend to be too complicated for most girls".

I sigh and try and not say out loud that he's said the magic word 'complicated'. Ever since reading Wuthering Heights as a teenager, I've had a thing for broody, damaged men.

Having dated a series of cheery, sporty boys introduced to me via my parents' social set, I can honestly say none of them even came close to this connection I have with Conor. I shrug off his comment with a fake laugh and say,

"Maybe I like complicated? Come on, let me see what the other rooms in this gorgeous cottage look like".

He hesitates and opens the door of the living room. He brings Mrs. Casey's photograph over to a cupboard, reaches into a drawer and finds some string which he attaches to the back of the photograph. I'm glad he is busy, so he won't notice the look of astonishment on my face. There are dozens of photographs on the wall. At the centre of the wall, is a photograph of a young teenage girl who is dark haired and pretty. She has one hand placed on her hip and she is gazing at the camera with a look in her eyes that spells trouble. I look through the photographs and I am sure I recognise some of the people in them. Conor hangs the photograph of Mrs. Casey on the left of the wall. I point to the photograph of the girl in the centre.

"That's my mother", Conor says quietly.

"They gave me that photo of her to take with me when the orphanage closed".

I look at the photos and admire the Christening photos, the birthday cakes, the Christmas mornings, the wedding photos, and it dawns on me that I do recognise the people. Conor has created a wall of photographs from all the deceased members of the nursing home. I look at him and realise that besides the photograph of his mother, none of the other people are related to him. He has invented a whole family for himself.

"They are my family. We might not be related but I loved them. All of them", Conor says firmly, but a little defensively.

We stand there holding hands and admire his fabricated family tree.

CHAPTER 10

ANGELA:

I'm in my dressing room, a bottle of vodka placed on my antique walnut dressing table. It is growing dark outside, and I can hear Matthew singing downstairs, something by U2, 'I still haven't found what I'm looking for', I think. That makes two of us. He is in his element – investors en route, the best booze lined up and platters of Mediterranean bite-sized treats laid out on the dining room table. I can smell candles lit – 'summer's eve' is becoming overpowered by 'bonhomie'. Walsh, O'Brien, and Hennessy will be arriving shortly in their beamers and mercs, leaving their wives to sit in with the kids. The wives probably have wine poured and drink it after bathing French designer labelled kids and putting them to bed in themed rooms. The women are in my social circle. We meet three or four times a week for lunch, cocktails, body wraps and charity fund-raisers. They are not my friends. No-one makes friends in this world. We align ourselves with the right people as it's all about being seen in the right place, doing the right thing with the right people. It's all about fake friendships, air kissing when we meet and in Matthew's case, flirting with love-starved wives on every occasion possible. I drink vodka and concentrate on the job in hand. I'm plucked, waxed and ready to go, like a turkey on Christmas Eve. We made a pact, Matthew, and I, after the first few years of our marriage, that I wasn't going to do this anymore, but from what I can gather from news bulletins and radio shows, the country is screwed, and Matthew needs this money.

'One more development, Ange and we're done', he says. He doesn't mean it though, because he is just as much an addict as the junkies he steps over in O'Connell Street. Money is his heroin. I swallow down my self-disgust with another slug of vodka. There you go, Ange, you are almost breathing normally. Breathe in. Breathe out. It's not that complicated. I look in the mirror and try and block out the thought that Matthew bought it for me on our honeymoon in a tiny village in Provence. It was such a pretty little village for a pretty little girl. Like me. Everyone says pretty girls have all the fun. I try not to vomit. Breathe in. Breathe out. Knock your vodka back in one go. Now that feels better. I look at myself in the mirror. My expensive hair looks good tonight. Well, it would want to be at two hundred euro every session.

'Nearly forty and still got it, Angela', that's what my trainer said. He stood there, a light sheen of sweat on his limbs, - you've still got it, looking good- and then the three killer words -for your age-in the gym, the other ladies slaying me with their eyes but saying, -Ah you are so gorgeous, Angela-

They moved in a pack towards me, like they were on an African plain and I was dinner. They were like hyenas if hyenas ever got to wear pastel coloured Lycra gym gear. 'Ha ha ha', they fake laughed. They've even learnt to laugh seductively; my pack of laughing, false nailed, spray-tanned, caramel highlighted hyena pretend friends. I apply mascara to make my lashes long, illustrious and some other scientific name which I read on the label. Make-up promises a lot but ends up in a dirty smudge on a piece of cotton wool at the end of the day. A bit like life if you think about it. The ladies won't like what you are up tonight, Angela, I think. They'll hunt you down for your duplicity. I drink more vodka and try not to destroy my 'Red carpet' glossy lipstick. I've got to stop at the two vodkas if I must fake being ladylike, for a few hours. The ladies will come to get you, Angela, I torture myself. I break my own rules and drink another half glass of vodka. Down the hatch, as Lizzy used to say. She with her Powers in a brown paper bag and me with my Miwadi,

"To us, sweetheart, two girls against the world", she'd say, and I'd tell her,

"I love you, Mam. Can we have crisps?", and she'd laugh

and say,

"We are so good together, Angela. But I'll find us a man to mind us soon".

You'd be so proud of me, Mam, tonight, standing in front of my honeymoon mirror in lingerie which cost more than our rent for a month.

I shiver. Don't think about Lizzy.

Dead dead dead dead dead.

She's not coming back to hold your hand, Angela. I slip the red dress over my head. Matthew told me to wear it. It is perfect for seduction for Walsh with the wandering hands which won't reach into his wallet to write the cheque for Matthew's new toy. Poor Matthew. Poor little rich boy Matthew who wants a new toy so Angela the doll-wife has to dress up prettily and get the new toy for poor little Matthew. I snort and realise the vodka is heading into my bloodstream too fast. I better stop drinking and go downstairs and eat some withered tomatoes soaked in aged balsamic vinegar. The vinegar makes me wish for chips and the pier at Howth where Lucy and I use to dangle our legs over, our lives in front of us and dazzling. I'm being consumed by the past tonight. I stand up and force myself to concentrate on what's ahead. I spray perfume on myself. Like a good girl. Good girl. Pretty girl. I wish I was ugly as a warthog so the hyenas and the men with fat hands would walk right past me. Beauty is a commodity which everyone wants to acquire. Matthew walks into the dressing room. He's wearing Hugo Boss and I can see myself in his shined-up shoes. Two red-laced Angela doll images are reflected back at me. I snort.

"Attractive, Angela. For fuck's sake, pull yourself together, babe", he says, as he takes the vodka bottle, pulls me towards him and kisses me.

"You look amazing, hon, I could…", he says in a husky tone, but his aftershave is scented to resemble wood shavings and gives me a hay fever type reaction and I sneeze all over his Hugo Boss suit. I drink my third vodka down in one go. I don't even bother with the tonic water this time. Matthew tries to clean the sneeze residue from his sleeve. I nearly laugh, but like the Queen of England, Matthew is not amused. Instead, I walk to the bathroom and fix my face. I join him back in front of our honeymoon mirror and say,

"Do you remember buying it for me?". His jaw clenches a bit. We loved each other then and I wish the mirror could become enchanted and show us the image we saw then - two bright-eyed honeymooners.

Matthew says nothing, but the muscle in his jaw clenches tighter and he falls back on his usual,

"You look amazing, Ange".

I sigh, watch him in the mirror and wonder if I ever really loved this man. I've always had a habit of confusing love with gratitude. Matthew tries to kiss me, but I step away from him and say,

"Don't kiss me when I have to do this shit".

He backs away and pretends to adjust his cufflinks.

"Last time", I tell him.

I sit on a stool and try to tie the buckles on my strappy and bejewelled sandals. Matthew kneels down as I'm having trouble with my task as my hand tremors slightly. He touches my feet gently and has to concentrate very hard to tie the minute buckles. He stays on his knees before me. We sit there for a while. Like a still life painting. And then the doorbell rings. And Matthew moves fast. There are voices full of laughter and I stand up. OK, Angela. You can do this. Walk down the stairs. One little step at a time.

The evening passes in a blur. Matthew surpasses himself.

If there was an award for debonair property developer host of the year, he'd win it. There is a lot of slapping of backs and as always, the masks slip and the men revert to the locker room conversations of their teenage years and there is a lot of talk about other people they deal with and women they want to bed. I paint a smile on my face and pour drinks, massage egos and give a lot of my attention to the reluctant Walsh. I press myself against him, touch his arm, seduce him with my layers of scientifically proven to be irresistible, mascaraed eyelashes and talk in a Hollywood starlet baby-like breathless voice. I disgust myself. I take a break to re-light candles and watch the men surround Matthew and talk about their new development and listen to their 'fuck the accountants' comments. Hennessy tells Matthew that his West Wharf development project is being called 'The Icarus Project'. The men laugh heartily but Matthew's smile is frozen on his face for a moment. I remind myself to google the word 'Icarus' later. My hasty departure from the school system has left me educationally deficient, but I am a fast learner and Google has become my own personal tutor. Matthew pours more drinks and looks right at me. It's time.

I turn up the music and dance. All eyes watch me. I'm becoming dizzy and faint, but I give it my best shot and somewhere in the vodka fueled dance, I lose myself. I disappear in my head and go somewhere else far from this elegant, sweat filled room. I can feel Walsh's eyes on me and only come to when I'm standing in the kitchen, pushed against the sink, his fingers ripping the expensive red lace of my dress. I hear Matthew talking quietly in the drawing room and wonder why he's leaving it so long. I fake appreciation of Walsh's rape-style foreplay and try hard not to remember that his wife is one of the nicer ones, the first one of the circle to invite me into her home.

"Take off the dress", Walsh says.

I slowly move one strap to appease him, but all the time I'm thinking, where the fuck is Matthew? It's quiet in the drawing room, just the murmur of male voices and jazz. Walsh is impatient and places his hands beneath my dress. He removes it for me. Just when I think I'll have to come out of character as the willing lover, the kitchen fills with light. And there he is. As rehearsed. Matthew. His hands are to his face, and he's got a look of horror on his face. Walsh is lost in the act, and it takes a moment for him to realise that Matthew is standing right behind him.

"James? What the fuck?".

Walsh steps away from me abruptly. I listen to his weak apologies, the 'I don't know what happened', the 'she led me on, Matthew'. I turn away from them and drink water from the tap. It feels clear and pure in the male hormone-soaked atmosphere. Matthew's hand is gentle on my shoulder.

"Are you alright, Angela?", he asks quietly.

"We've all had too much to drink. James, go through to the

drawing room and I'll just leave you boys to talk", I say, my voice small and mean.

"Did he hurt you?", Matthew asks, his eyes on Walsh.

"No, no, well, not much. I'll dab a little arnica cream on the bruises. Sure, look they are going already", I lie.

Walsh is beside himself, a look of terror on his face. Matthew kisses me on the forehead and says,

"You go up to bed, sweetheart. I'll come up to you in a while, bring you a hot chocolate, maybe".

I almost laugh as the hot chocolate is a bit of overkill. Matthew walks up to Walsh and slaps him on the back. Walsh is relieved, but suspicious.

"It's fine. James. Nothing to worry about. Angela is discreet and she won't say anything to Marian, sure you won't Angela?".

I sigh and do my best imitation of a wounded deer.

"No, let's just forget it happened. You boys get your deal sorted. Signed and sealed. And I promise, James, I'll be fine. I'm not sure I could cope with the police tonight".

Matthew puts his arm around the stunned Walsh and by the time they leave the kitchen, Walsh has sealed his fate on the so-called 'Icarus Project'. The ill-timed pressing of flesh against a kitchen sink has cost him three million Euro. Walsh's wife, Marian, is the wealthy one in their marriage and he is keen to keep her on side and rumour has it that she is getting a little impatient with his reputation for sleeping with women all over Dublin. I kick off my sandals and walk upstairs. The shame increases with each step. I walk to the bathroom and decontaminate myself, put the red dress and expensive lingerie in the pedal pin, wrap myself in a large dressing gown and decide to treat myself. I walk to the bedside locker in my room, find the key and smile. My little secret. I ignore the sound of male voices below me and leave them to their hangover inducing drinking. I walk to the end of the corridor. To the guest room. I've been keeping it a secret for a while. Matthew is never home much these days and the pastel paints and delicate fabrics arrived without his detection. I open the door and sit on the chintz decorated armchair. I wrap a patchwork quilt around me. I pick up a children's book and read it, lost in the world of rabbits and sweet girls with names I love. I switch on the lamp and marvel at the sun, moon and stars illuminated on the pale lemon walls. I sleep there until dawn breaks. In my baby's nursery.

CHAPTER 11

MARTHA:

I have been having strange dreams since discovering the old graveyard. I woke last night from a dream where my mother stood to the side of the graveyard and said in a very quiet voice – You, be careful, Martha, the dead are restless-. She was wearing a jade silk gown which she kept for major performances, and she was beautiful although her skin was blue-tinged. I awoke with all my bed sheets tangled, visited the kitchen to pour a glass of ice-cold water and while there I opened my laptop. I googled the phrase from Conor's tattoo – veritatem voluntas ex- and discovered that it is Latin and means 'the truth will out'. I sat by the open window of the kitchen, enjoying the scent of salt from the sea and wondered what truth needed to be told and whether it should remain where it was, hidden and secret. I remembered Mum's face in the dream and her finger pressed to her lips requesting silence and felt torn between my old and new love. I arrive to my shift, a little ragged around the edges, feeling tearful and confused.

Martina notices my mood and asks me what's happened to dim my smile. I thank her for being kind and say I have been watching too many late-night movies when a girl should be getting some beauty sleep. She laughs and says I don't require any more beauty sleep, that I am beautiful enough. I touch her hand and thank her, trying to smile brightly but can feel tears prickling. I find kindness can do that, undo a person. I decide to visit Peter first on my rounds. There is a commotion in the corridor, and I find myself being lifted high by male hands – Tony- kissed on the cheek and placed back down in front of a jubilant group. I fix my hair and attempt to straighten down my uniform. Tony pins me to the wall and I think of Dad's rare butterflies captured in a glass frame, covered in thick glass. I long for some thick glass to protect myself from Tony. He is in a great mood and points to the smiling group with him and tells me,

"We passed our exams, Martha. Brains and muscles, huh?".

He flexes the muscles in his arms and places one of my hands on them. He leans in close to me until I can smell his aftershave and asks,

"We are going to celebrate after work, tomorrow maybe. Now that we can all move up the pay scale. Have you seen your boyfriend today?".

He says 'boyfriend' in the same way that someone would

say 'tax bill' or 'plane crash'. I peel myself away from him and his muscles and reply,

"I presume you are talking about Conor. A. He isn't my boyfriend and B. No, I've only just arrived, so I haven't seen him yet".

His group of merry men dissipate, and I walk towards Peter's room, ignoring the fact that Tony persists in accompanying me. He hums out of tune as he walks and bows as we get to the door of Peter's room and says loudly,

"Ladies first".

I walk past him and mutter 'for fuck's sake'.

Conor sits with Peter reading from 'The Selfish Giant' book. I plump up Peter's pillows and fix his blanket which has come loose from the bed.

"Hi Martha", Conor says shyly, and he helps me tuck in the blanket.

"Hi yourself", I reply and Peter smiles and winks at me.

"A bad night, Peter? We'll have you sorted in no time, won't we Conor? Maybe a bit of a walk to the garden later. You could probably do with a bit of nicotine? I mean, fresh air".

He laughs and his eyes though tired, are kind. Tony walks up to the bed and makes his presence known. He tries to high five Conor, but it becomes awkward when Conor drops the book on the floor. Tony asks him in a fake friend manner,

"Are we still on for having a few drinks or twenty in your place tomorrow night? You know, for the exam results. Be a bit of craic, huh, Conor? Did you get yours back yet? We'll all let our hair down. Martha, you'll come too, won't you?".

Conor hesitates and says,

"Did I agree to that? I don't remember. But if Martha comes, maybe that's OK, then".

Tony flinches slightly, walks away and says,

"OK, Conor, about 9.30 tomorrow night. Let's just keep schtum about it. We don't want Gerard finding out. He's such a fucking woman sometimes. Everyone's broke so a few cans in yours would be a great way to celebrate. See you there, Martha".

He winks at me and then leaves. We are all silent until Peter says,

"Rory O'Driscoll".

Conor and I look at each other, a little confused and Peter continues,

"Rory O'Driscoll. Atlantic Ballroom. 1955. Tried to steal my Margaret from me. Right in front of my eyes. Blackguard. But I was having none of it. I had spent weeks practising waltzing techniques with my mother in the kitchen each night after work. Took a few days to stop maiming her feet. But it paid off. Rory O'Driscoll may have had the looks, hair greased back and a new suit straight off the rails at Clery's. But when he danced with Margaret, he stood on her toes. And she said he had no rhythm whatsoever. You can tell a lot about a man from the way he dances, Margaret said. I asked her to dance after she'd finished a waltz with Rory O'Driscoll. I must have been an OK dancer. She married me ten months later. Love whispers before it shouts".

He is tired after his reverie, and he looks fondly at Conor who is slightly embarrassed. I finish tucking the blanket in an attempt to leave, saying,

"You have a nice nap Peter, and I'll see you later with Conor for your walk".

He smiles at me, and Conor continues to read,

"Then the Spring came, and all over the country there were little blossoms and little birds...'

Peter sleeps for a long while, hopefully dreaming of his wife, Margaret, who recognised a good man when she saw him and learnt the value of a great dance partner. I check all my other patients while Peter is sleeping and am just on the way to Gerard's office when I knock on Mrs. Quinn's door. I can't see her sitting in her usual armchair so knock gently on her bathroom door. She opens the door and I try not to laugh as I see that she is attempting to dye her hair a brunette shade.

"I'm making a bags of this, Martha", she says, white hand towels dripping with dye on her tiny shoulders.

"Let me help", I say to her, and we spend a happy hour turning her into not quite the 'Cheryl' shade she had been hoping for when she bought the hair-dye, but near enough if you don't look closely. Mrs. Quinn is delighted with her almost 'Cheryl' hairdo and says that she does it mainly to keep the 'awesome' comments coming from her grandson. I blow her a kiss, as she brushes her hair at her dressing table and walk to Gerard's office. The door to his office is shut. This is an unusual event, as Gerard has an open-door policy and believes in -transparent communication and interaction between caregivers and management-phrases borrowed from his many training courses, I'd hazard a guess. I take a seat outside Gerard's office and try to leaf through magazines and ignore the voices rising from his office. The voices become louder followed a moment later by Gerard's voice sounding low and full of reassurance. There is a sudden burst of noise, and the door opens abruptly, and Conor walks briskly through it, stops suddenly when he sees me, mutters a quiet 'oh, hi, Martha' and then walks away. Gerard stands at the door, a concerned look on his face and calls after Conor,

"I'm so sorry, Conor. My hands are tied here. It's just the way it works nowadays. We'll talk....".

He doesn't finish his sentence as Conor is long gone. Gerard runs his fingers through his greying hair and smiles at me with his sharp, blue eyes.

"Martha. Thanks for coming. You are going to help me with all this paperwork?".

He gestures towards a desk filled with large piles of folders and groans mournfully.

"Inspections. They've got to be done, but Christ the amount of box-ticking it involves is unreal".

We spend the next few hours or so sorting through the paperwork and it's only when we take a coffee break at his desk, I ask,

"Don't answer me if it's none of my business. But is everything OK with Conor?".

He leans back in his chair and says,

"Martha, I know you two are close, so you might be able to help him. He didn't pass the Carer's exam. You know, the one that the assistants need to work directly with patients?".

"What does that mean for him, exactly?", I ask.

"It means that he can only do general jobs around here now. He can't work directly with the patients. That's just the way it is nowadays, Martha. It's all box ticking, dotting the i's and health and safety. I know it's all good for everyone but in Conor's case, the system works against him. Between you and me, I don't think he will ever pass the exam. Let's just say he's had a difficult educational background", Gerard replies.

"But he's the best assistant by far. The residents love him and get irritated when they have to have someone else", I say,

"Martha, there's nothing I can do. As I said to Conor, it's not my decision. My hands are tied".

He holds his hands up in the air, in a surrender gesture
and passes some more files to me, indicating that our
conversation is over. I am sorting through some old files,
and I am so preoccupied with what he said about Conor,
that at first, I don't notice the old, battered envelope placed
between a batch of invoices. I open the envelope gently
and remove some old photographs from it. They are
slightly faded but are full of images of the same children. I
look at one of the photographs and smile at the laughing
faces in it. About thirty young children stand formally with a
group of staff outside the building we now work in. I can
see the sign with *St. Jude's Children's Home* written on it.
Gerard walks over to me, stands behind my chair, and
says,

"That was the last group photograph they took of them. It
was run by the nuns originally but by the early 90's it was
privately owned and nearly out of operation. We took it
over in 2001 and gutted the place. That photograph gives
me shivers every time I see it. Something so sad about it,
even with their happy little faces in it".

Gerard walks back to his desk. I am drawn to a pair of
boys who stand slightly aloof in the photograph, their
heads turned towards each other- one dark, one blonde.
They smile at each other, and you can tell that they are
great friends, because even in such a faded photograph,
their body language indicates their close friendship. I sigh
as I look at them and something about the dark-haired boy
makes me look again at him.

"Gerard? Have you got a second? That's Conor? I am nearly sure".

He walks back over to my desk and says,

"Yes. He was here when we came here. He slipped through the cracks in the system and when the home was sold, he somehow managed to avoid detection. The place was emptied in 1997, all the children were gone by then, except for Conor. He stayed here with a caretaker staff till 2001 when we bought it. By then, he was sixteen and nobody knew what to do with him. So, I just gave him a job and offered him the gate lodge to live in. Poor kid, he was such a lost soul".

I look at some other photographs and ask,

"How come he was never adopted?".

Gerard sighs and replies as he walks away,

"He said that no-one ever wanted him".

I look at the photographs again, then put them in a file with 'The Saint Jude Children' written on it in a clear, tidy font and file it among the 2001 invoices. I have a strong feeling I'll be coming back for it.

CHAPTER 12

MATTHEW:

Angela played a blinder. Walsh wept into his whiskey and did a great little 'I don't know what came over me, Matthew' act for two hours that I will never get back in my life but hey, at one point five mill an hour, I wasn't exactly complaining. I got the whole sob story about what would happen if his rich wife discovered one more incident involving him and a woman. He was on his last chance, and he didn't want to blow the lifestyle she had mainly provided for him up till now. She had told him that she would cut him off with nothing and make him pay if she heard one more story about him. She was pissed off with the humiliation he caused her. I played the cuckolded husband until I got bored with it. It was me mentioning the possibility that Angela may have taken a photograph, but I was sure that she could delete it, that shut him up in the end. I forgave him at four o'clock in the morning as I couldn't listen to the little weasel for one more minute. I sent him home in a taxi because I didn't want him drink-driving and wrapped around a pole before he had a chance to press send to his bank on his laptop. The money pinged into my account at eleven a.m. the following day. I told Laura to bring in some champagne and we sat watching Dublin through the window, clinking crystal flutes. She tried the flirty secretary act on me again, twenty-four years old with a first-class business degree and a crush on me that was embarrassing for her. There has only ever been Angela for me. I don't count the occasional nights in hotels with bored females looking for a quick shag as being unfaithful. I'm only human for fuck's sake and there's only so much "Oh, you look like Colin Farrell" that I can take before I'm tempted. I only sleep with women when I'm out of this country. My infidelity is based on geographical opportunities. I married Angela on Irish soil, so I am faithful to her here. It makes sense if you twist your morals just a little bit. I sent Laura back to her desk with a quick retort of,

"Find someone at your own level, Laura. Aim a little lower, sweetheart".

You would think that would be enough to get her typing up her C.V. at high speed, but she is addicted to me. Like Angela. I walk past Laura later in the morning, hand her a bouquet of flowers and say,

"Sorry, sweetheart, if I was a bit harsh. But you know, you are way too valuable to me to ruin our relationship with sex".

Her cheeks flush with shame and I can't hear what she says, but she'll be fine, until the next time anyway. I walk to my office, check the account for West Wharf and look at all the zeroes. One hundred apartments and space for retail units. I make a note to change the spec to one hundred and twenty apartments. The architect will have a hissy fit but so what, if some buyers only have one window facing the car park. They will have the ultimate prize, a prime city-centre Dublin address. They won't have time to look out their one window anyway, they'll be too busy working to pay their mortgages. I ring my accountant and arrange to meet him for lunch. I'm keen to get the balance of the finance arranged for the development to get off the ground. I'll need at least twice what I've raised already to get the rest of the cash sorted to make this project viable. O' Dwyer sounds like he's in a bad mood so I play the chummy old school buddy that he thinks I am and tell him,

"My shout today. Go crazy and have whatever you want".

"Too fucking right", he barks back at me.

I put the phone down and try not to acknowledge a nagging feeling in my brain, which is trying to tell me that something wasn't quite right in the accountant's tone. It's all the talk on the radio about economic warnings and phrases like 'belly-up' and 'overheating' being bandied about by everyone that has me doubting myself today. Doubt is something I don't do, as a rule. I make myself some coffee and look out of my floor length window in the direction of West Wharf. I imagine all the money it'll make me and wonder what I'll do with it. There are only so many cars you can drive out of a showroom before it all gets a bit tired. Maybe I should get into boats? A yacht for the weekends out in Dun Laoghaire? Or fuck it, think bigger, Matthew, Monte Carlo? I am daydreaming about being at the helm of a boat and can almost feel the sun on my face when a text pings on my phone,

-3pm? We still on? Ax-

Fuck it. The fertility clinic. My part of the deal. I don't reply. I sit at my desk and organise a folder for my meeting with O' Dwyer and am sitting there for ten minutes sipping a five Euro glass of water at the bar, when he arrives, wearing our old school tie and the same navy suit he's been wearing for the last ten years.

"Drink, Brian?", I gesture towards the bar.

"Yes. No., I'll stay sober. I might need to for this. I hope you've booked us somewhere private".

We sit in a booth at the back of the restaurant, eating prawns and sipping tap water, which has been renamed something French, when O' Dwyer casually ruins my entire life. He has a tragic expression on his face and mayonnaise on his tie and I will the words that come out of his mouth to be different. I throw some money at him and leave the restaurant as fast as I can. I can hear O' Dwyer's nasal voice as I put on my coat,

"Matthew, Matthew".

I ignore the whining and walk out onto the street, momentarily blinded by the Spring sunshine. I don't want to head back to the office, and I certainly don't want to go to the fertility clinic with a little jar and some magazines to please Angela and her obsessional baby craziness. I walk to St. Stephen's Green and ignore the junkies asking me for cash. Parasites, I think, get a job like the rest of us. Or at least, buy some deodorant. I can't find a bench to sit on, so I make do with sitting on the grass in front of the pond and watch a woman and her kids feed the ducks. The kids go through two bags of breadcrumbs and still the greedy ducks look for more. One of the kids starts crying and says,

"But we don't have any left".

But the greedy ducks don't care. They want more and more, and they swim off to find someone else who will give it to them, leaving the small boy forlorn and staring into his empty breadcrumb-less bag.

"You are over-extended, Matthew. You still owe the bank six point three on the Ballsbridge project and those units are not shifting. This West Wharf money you received is only half of what you need for it. The Bank is not going to lend you the rest of it to develop the whole site You're going to have to have to come up with the balance yourself. And two of your own apartment buildings have only a third of full occupancy each, so you need to hustle and get those units filled. People have pulled out because they're nervous of over-extending. Overall, you are sailing close to the wind, Matthew. You need to slow down, maybe take stock".

O' Dwyer kept talking, his mouth moved but I stopped listening and left. I'm sure the little weasel who makes money from every single deal I painstakingly put together, has all his cash tucked away somewhere safe. People like him don't take chances. They wait for me to make them money and then run for the hills the minute it all goes pear-shaped. I'm going to sack the fucker. In two minutes, I'll leave here and go back to the office and face the music. For the moment, I'll stay here with the ducks. Watch them wait for more breadcrumbs. Someone else will come along. They always do.

CHAPTER 13

ANNA:

Thank God, I haven't seen Lucy since. I haven't the
strength to deal with her. I will, soon. I put my key in the
door of the flat, close it and sit in the dark of my sitting
room. I don't open the curtains. For someone who always
loved the light and bright sunshine of Spain, I prefer the
half-light these days. My body is sore. Every ancient bit of
it. Face up to it, Anna. Get a grip. God, I'd give anything for
someone to make me a cup of tea. Arthur or that gobshite
nephew. But they're all gone. I'm no more use to anyone.
So be it. I make myself get up and face the kitchen. It
smells of the sausages I burnt last night, which I cooked
and didn't even eat. So sorry. So sincerely sorry. So
absolutely sincerely sorry. That poor young doctor having
to tell me.

Spread.

All over.

Into your bones.

You are rotten with cancer, Anna. Is basically what she said. Poor girl, in her lemon dress, all crisp and fresh like a summer flower. And me with my spread all over cancer, dressed in my black slacks and grey jumper, like winter, in her lovely office full of degrees and diplomas framed on the wall. Oh, what a lovely life she'll have.

"No, thanks, I won't have treatment. I'll take my punishment", I said.

"It's not punishment", she replied. And she looked shocked. Poor young girl. From a house that smelt of baked bread all her childhood, I'd say. Piano lessons and midnight picnics. She makes me feel good just to sit in the rays of goodness that surround her.

"Well, I disagree", I said. "This is my punishment. I'll take it and work with it".

She ran out of words then. Pressed leaflets on me. Lovely little bundles of paper with diagrams on them. Not one mention of death in them. I read them in the taxi on the way home and disposed of them in the bin on the way through the flats.

You're not thinking straight, she said, the lovely doctor in the lemon dress. Oh yes, I am, I replied. What goes around comes around. I looked over to the window beside the doctor and Lizzy nodded 'yes'. You see, even Lizzy knows it's my due. I will rest a while. Then, I need to sort a few things out. I'll just drink my tea first.

CHAPTER 14

ANGELA:

I wake up to the sound of birdsong, a good omen. Today is the day. Matthew is a reluctant father, that much is true. He'll be fine once he sees the baby when it eventually comes. We've just spent too long together as a couple; lunching, brunching, and jetting off for luxurious five-star city breaks. All those cities seem the same after a while; petals on beds, Egyptian thread counts, cocktails in quirky bars, boutiques with pushy sales assistants selling this season's hot dress and handbags. All that glisters is not gold. I have become a woman who knows that 'glisters' is the right word to use in that phrase. I spend a lot of time sitting at a desk in my small office off the kitchen, surrounded by books which I've ordered from the internet. I hide them under glossy women's magazines so that Matthew at a quick glance will think I'm immersed in the frenzy of finding a new frilly frock. Instead, I read poetry, history, art and classics. Half of the time I don't really understand what's in these books. I keep reading anyway, as it's daunting how much a woman needs to know if she is to keep up with this new world she has found herself in. I walk to my office and open a book on Greek myths. The Icarus comment from Matthew's colleagues has made me curious. I first had to Google it to even find out that Icarus is a character from a Greek myth.

I sip green tea as I need to be calm today and leaf through the hardback book, admiring the illustrations and I'm content that by reading stuff like this, I can attempt to unlock the secrets of this world of educated people I find myself in. They are casual with their education, take it as a given that it is there for the taking for them. Ivy clad buildings all over the city await them and their offspring to welcome them into this world full of power, cash and rules I have had to learn. If you are determined enough, you can become chameleon-like and appear to be one of them. I have spent twenty years cramming here at my desk; peering at old maps and reading poetry, history and science books just to keep up. I find a lot of the education is wasted on them as they are consumed with the same desires as everyone else, clothes, cars, holidays and houses. As Oscar Wilde would say, they know the price of everything and the value of nothing. I love Oscar Wilde and he has been one of my favourites to study.

I open my Greek mythology book and breathe in the scent of ink and paper. I read of the fate of Icarus.

Icarus was the young son of Daedalus and Nafsicrate, one of King Minos' servants. Daedalus was way too smart and inventive; thus, he started thinking how he and Icarus would escape the Labyrinth. Knowing that his architectural creation was too complicated, he figured out that they could not come out on foot. He also knew that the shores of Crete were perfectly guarded, thus, they would not be able to escape by sea either. The only way left was the air. Daedalus managed to create gigantic wings, using branches of osier and connected them with wax. He taught Icarus how to fly but told him to keep away from the sun because the heat would make the wax melt, destroying the wings. Daedalus and Icarus managed to escape the Labyrinth and flew to the sky, free. The flight of Daedalus and Icarus was the first time that man managed to fight the laws of nature and beat gravity. Although he was warned, Icarus was too young and too enthusiastic about flying. He got excited by the thrill of flying and carried away by the amazing feeling of freedom and started flying high to salute the sun, diving low to the sea, and then up high again. His father Daedalus was trying in vain to make young Icarus to understand that his behaviour was dangerous, and Icarus soon saw his wings melting. Icarus fell into the sea and drowned.

I feel a bit sorry for the father, Daedalus, and how his love for his son, brought him to such loss. I also feel a tinge of regret for the month that Matthew and I spent sailing around the Greek coast, in a luxury yacht three summers ago. All that time wasted preening myself with the other wives; dressed in leopard skin bikinis and listening to them talking in whispery baby voices to their elderly husbands. I should have jumped off the ship and learnt something. I close the book and file the information in my brain. You wouldn't need to be a Professor of Economics in Trinity College to combine the Icarus project comment with the non-stop financial talk on the radio. It's becoming hysterical and I can sense among my acquired social set that the bubble is about to burst. There is already a lot of talk among the women about holidays being cancelled and cars not being upgraded. They have a certain panicked look in their eyes, but they are queens of self-protection and will not air their doubts in public. That would be social suicide. I tidy up my workspace and place this month's Vogue on top of the desk, admiring the silk dress which is this season's must-have. I have it already in my wardrobe, in three different colours, none of which I've tried on yet.

I pack up my Audi convertible and put some gifts in the boot for Amy and Jason. I've got to stop buying them gifts as Lucy will kill me and as she said herself, they've no space left in their toy boxes. I'm just about to leave when I remember the item in my wardrobe which I have forgotten, run back up the stairs, pack the envelope in my handbag and leave for Lucy's. I sit outside her house for a minute as I can hear her in the back garden from here. She is chastising Amy for pinching baby Jason, and I can hear tiredness in her voice, but it's laden with love. Funny to think that I, Angela, married to Matthew Kennedy and who lives in one of Ireland's most desired addresses, could envy Lucy her ex-corporation house in Raheny, with her garden full of red roses and kid's toys. I love Lucy way too much to be truly envious. She walks around the side of the house and spots me. She is wearing denim shorts and a red t-shirt with *Sexy mama* printed on it. Her hair is loose and although she complains constantly of being overweight, I think she looks like one of the women in a French painting in the Art Gallery, vital and ripe.

"Are you going to sit there all day, Angela? Or are you going to come in and help me power wash these two?", she says, pointing to her mud-encrusted kids.

I help her wash and change them, first of all putting her apron on.

"White linen? Jesus, Angela, you'll be destroyed", she said when she saw my trouser suit.

We wash the kids and dress them in little dungarees and after we've left them safe and clean in the sitting room watching a purple dinosaur telling them how to be caring, we eat our lunch. Lucy has outdone herself with lunch. She must have bought half of the items on the deli counter in the supermarket where she works most evenings. She places the feast on the toy-littered kitchen table where I sit facing the fridge which has handprints and school art plastered all over it. I think of my stainless-steel American fridge which makes ice and has nothing but a few yoghurts

in it and bottles of white wine in varying degrees of
fullness. Lucy watches me and says,

"Enough now, Angela. This is your chance today. It's a
good day. OK?".

I smile a half smile and push some coleslaw around my
plate, my appetite gone and tension building. I put my fork
down and say,

"I went back to my old tricks the other night, Lucy".

Lucy is quiet and continues to empty her nearly cleared
plate. She reaches over to my plate and spears some
prawn cocktail onto her fork, and I know she is buying time.
She has a habit of over-eating when stressed.

"Why, Ange? I thought you and Matthew were done with all
that crap. It was something that you did at the beginning
when you didn't know any better and wanted to keep him
because you didn't want to go back to that shit life you
were having. Sleeping with his clients and then
tranquilizing him with sex all the time. Makes me crazy
every time I think of it. You know he doesn't deserve you.
You have it all wrong. You think he owns you."

I say,

"Lucy, I know. I just had to keep him on side for today. You know he doesn't want kids really. I just did what I had to do. It'll be worth it. Promise".

"You have one fucked up marriage, Ange, but I'll say no more. Today, anyway", she says and just as she starts to lecture me again, the baby monitor comes to life and she goes into check on the kids, forgetting that I can hear her as she talks to Amy.

"You are going to go to university, do you hear me? And not end up like Aunty Ange and me, doing shit for the rest of your life. Do you hear me? No stupid shift jobs or doing what Aunty Ange does. You earn your own money, Amy. OK?".

I pick up the receiver end of the monitor from a kitchen shelf and walk to the sitting room where Lucy sits, her two kids competing to sit on her lap and say,

"I can hear you, you know, Lucy", and place the monitor on the sofa arm.

"I know you can", she replies, and she switches off the monitor on the other side of the room, her two kids attached to her like little monkeys.

Amy looks at me and says,

"What does Aunty Ange do that I shouldn't do? She's very pretty and smells like flowers and has lots of nice stuff".

Lucy sighs, strokes her hair and says,

"She's like a woman in a country and western song. Stands by her man".

Amy looks confused and Lucy starts to sing in a nasal tone, doing her best Tammy Wynette impersonation.

"Sometimes it's hard to be a woman, giving all your love to just one man. You'll have bad times. And he'll have good times…".

She sings the rest of it and the kids start to drift off to sleep. I say to her,

"Very funny, Lucy. You should give up the cash-office job in the supermarket and enter the X Factor. Simon Cowell would love your back story".

She doesn't laugh. She doesn't like my life, one bit. Amy and Jason have fallen fast asleep, and I help her place blankets over their tiny little shapes on the sofa, kiss them both on the forehead and whisper,

"I nearly forgot. I've brought gifts for them. I'll just pop to the car and get them".

We close the door to the sitting room, walk to my Audi and Lucy laughs when she sees it.

"I thought Matthew told you to drive the cleaner's Mini when you come to visit me. He won't be impressed. He'll think it'll be robbed and halfway across the city, to be sold by the time we've had coffee".

I smile and say, 'fuck him' and take the gifts for the kids out of the car and Lucy utters her usual,

"Oh, no, Angela, you have them ruined".

We walk back into the house, and I remove an envelope from my handbag and ask her if she can put it with the rest. We walk up to the attic where Lucy shimmies up a precarious looking loft ladder and hides my envelope with the others.

"One of these days, I'm going to ask you why you are putting wads of cash in my attic, Angela, but not today".

I help her manoeuvre the attic stairs back into position and we walk back downstairs and into to her garden, to sit and soak up a few rays of sun. Lucy is restless and says,

"What time is your appointment, Angela?".

I look at my watch and say,

"3 p.m. I'd better get my act together and go".

We both rise and I freshen up in Lucy's family bathroom, smiling at the bath full of plastic animals as I re-apply make-up and spray perfume on my wrists. Lucy walks me to the car, hugs me and says,

"I hope it all goes well, Angela. I'll be praying for you. I lit two candles this morning in the church, and you know how much of an effort that was for me as I'm allergic to religion".

I hug her back, get into my car and say,

"Thanks, hon. Don't worry. I have a good feeling about this. Really. I do".

Lucy fidgets as I put on my seatbelt and I ask her,

"What's up with you, Lucy? I know you too well. There's something on your mind. Come on, spit it out?".

She stands on the road and plays with her hair, a habit she's had since I first knew her.

"No, Angela, not today. I'll tell you another day. You just go".

I sigh and say,

"No, now you have me worried. Are you sick? There's nothing wrong with Dave, is there? Or Jesus, one of the kids?".

She interrupts me to say,

"No, sorry, Angela. Everyone is fine".

"What is it then, Lucy? Come on tell me?".

Lucy looks at her feet and says in a very quiet voice,

"God. I didn't want to tell you today, but I'm just going to have to now. Anna's back".

I don't reply. I wave at her, start my car and drive to the fertility clinic.

CHAPTER 15

MARTHA:

The sun is shining through the windows of Conor's cottage. I'm helping him set up for the party tonight. I am reluctant to do it, as I know what Tony and his mates are capable of and it would be just like them to wreck Conor's place and ruin things for him. I struggle to see why he agreed to do it. Maybe he's like Dad, who is like a demon possessed at the moment, decorating the mews with manic energy which keeps him there from dawn to dusk each day. Mary, our housekeeper, said to leave him at it. She says it is giving him a purpose and keeps him from under her feet each day. "And you'll have a lovely mews at the end of it all", she says, ever practical is our Mary. Maybe Conor just wants to move on, too. I clean the sitting room surfaces and constantly find my eyes being drawn to the photographs on the wall. I look at the photo of the girl who is Conor's mother and admire her posture and the way she looks so confidently at the camera, her chin tilted defiantly and her green eyes full of laughter. I can't help wondering how old she was when she gave birth to Conor and why she had to part with him. I dust the photographs and remind myself that I know nothing of the world. I am just a twenty-two-year-old nurse from a sea-side house with views of the Irish sea. I've become impatient with my own little world and feel an immersion into reality would do me no harm.

Conor walks back into the cottage, and I step away from the wall of photos and pretend I'm a 1950s housewife and look in cupboards to see what food I can prepare for tonight. Conor walks over to the sink, washes his hands and as I stand to greet him, I say,

"I hope you don't mind me asking, but why are you letting them have the party here? You know what Tony is like".

Conor finishes his glass of water and replies,

"I thought I was going to pass the exam too. And I thought that maybe for once, I'd try and be normal and have drinks with people. Do that weird thing that everyone else does. Socialize?".

I smile and say,

"Normal can be over-rated, in my opinion. I still think they are going to wreck the place, but sure let's do it and 'partaaay' as Tony keeps saying all day in that American voice he puts on. He's been watching too much of those American teen movies when they go on Spring break and drink yards of ale or whatever they put in it".

Conor laughs and I continue to open and close cupboards. He asks me,

"What are you looking for exactly?".

"Emm….not sure. I don't think it's going to be a jelly and ice-cream party, somehow or other. They are the only parties I know how to prepare. Mum always had caterers for parties in my house. Cutesy little mini-quiches and cocktails with olives in them".

Conor smiles and says,

"Sounds lovely, Martha. You must miss her?".

I manage to muster up my best stiff upper lip impression and and reply,

"Yes. Every day. But not as much as my father does. He's devastated".

He touches me briefly on the cheek and I become flustered and try to change the subject by saying,

"You are a bit like the soldier on Christmas day in the war?".

Conor looks puzzled.

"You know? He kicked the ball from behind the English line and into no-man's land. And then they had a ceasefire and played football all day on Christmas Day?".

"OK. So, I'm the English soldier? And Tony is the German?".

We both laugh and I say,

"Exactly. Tonight, we'll play football together. And tomorrow he'll go back to trying to gun you down".

I watch as Conor starts his motorbike outside to travel to the village nearby to fetch some provisions for tonight. I finish my own haphazard preparations and decide that it'll be fine to throw a few bags of crisps and nuts at the guests tonight. I look for some candles to bring atmosphere to the party. I climb up on a chair to reach the higher cupboard as I'm sure I saw some candles in there earlier. I feel a stab of jealousy in my heart as I think of Chloe, the pretty American girl, who must have bought them for a romantic dinner, maybe, or to place in Conor's bedroom, which I haven't seen yet. I get distracted, don't concentrate properly and dislodge a cardboard box which is wedged in beside the lilac candles. As I try to stop the box from falling, I stumble slightly, and I fall off the chair and the box and candles land right beside me on the ground. I curse myself for being so awkward and pick up the candles and put them on the counter. I pick up the box and set it on the kitchen table, intending to tape it back together, before I put it back where it was stored. The box is old and slightly dented and has the word, Odlums, printed on it with a picture of a happy family, one boy and one girl, merrily tucking into bowls of porridge. It has opened in the fall to the ground and a tiny piece of woollen fabric is visible. I take it out of the box and admire the yellowing miniature cardigan that appears to be hand-knitted. Tiny flowers are embroidered on the edge of it and stop short as if the knitter ran out of wool. I fold it gently and feel a certain guilt as I'm invading Conor's privacy and place it back in the box. I smile at the wholesome family who are so content together starting their day the Odlums way. As I place the cardigan back in the box, I feel the sharp coldness of metal. I remove the item, an old-fashioned Sheriff's badge, like one my cousins had when we spent hours in the garden when we were little. I pick up a torn scrap of faded paper and wonder what the writing on it means – 93 D and numbers which are hard to read. I hear Conor's motorbike outside in the lane, climb up on the chair once again and put the box and its mysterious contents away. I'm placing the candles in jam jars when he arrives in, laden with beer and crisps and he smiles as he sees my attempt to decorate his home.

"Did you get everything?", I ask him, slightly out of breath after my frantic attempts to decorate rapidly, having spent too much time on my Nancy Drew investigations.

"Beer, crisps, nuts", he replies, and we sit down and rest for a moment.

"Oh", I say, "I forgot to give you this, Conor. Now, don't look too closely".

I reach into my handbag and hand him the piece of embroidery that I completed for Mrs. Casey. He smiles at the kittens in an Easter basket, kindly not mentioning that we can both see exactly where Mrs. Casey's expert stitching finished and mine took over.

"It's the thought that counts", I say, and he places his finger on the stitches that I completed and says,

"I'm not used to getting presents. I'm not sure what to say, Martha".

I reply,

"I wouldn't exactly call it a present. But I did my best. Come on, let's hang it somewhere nice in the kitchen".

He stands very close to me as we place it on a wall, puts his arms around me and kisses me on the mouth. I kiss him back.

CHAPTER 16

ANGELA:

I drive like a lunatic from Lucy's to the city centre. I play a game with the traffic lights all the way into town. If they are green, everything is going to be perfect. The fertility expert will tell me I have the most beautiful womb ever.

"Well done, Angela, for having such a beautiful womb", he says in my reverie, sounding like Morgan Freeman for some reason. "We just need to sort out your husband's agile sperm, (cue image of tadpole like creatures wearing Nike trainers) and mix it altogether and voilà…".

(I am doubting if Morgan Freeman would say voilà, he doesn't strike me as being pretentious, but this is my reverie and I'll allow French posturing).

"…in nine months, out will come a perfect baby".

It's a shame the traffic lights don't co-operate. I've had more red lights than green and ignore the amber ones like everyone else does. I pass by the North Strand and pry my eyes away from the flats. It makes my driving erratic, but I cannot entertain the idea of allowing that spectre from my past, Anna, into my brain today.

-you be a good girl and do what you're told-

she says in a memory that's trying very hard to escape out of a space in my head.

Lucy has texted me at least six times since I left her house, and I don't reply. Anna can stay buried in my brain, all five foot one of that bee-hived excuse for a woman. I concentrate on getting to the clinic, conscious that I have lost all my green-tea calm, open the dashboard pocket, remove a C.D. from it and place it into the C.D. player. I listen to whale song as I drive into the car park of the exclusive clinic (discretion promised) and find the whales aren't dispelling my anxiety today. Instead, I have a large knot of anxiety building up in my stomach, eject the whales from the CD player, turn off the ignition, close my eyes and will myself to breathe deeply. I walk into the reception area of the clinic, noting the calm chic of the décor. The walls are covered in muted pastel French Impressionist paintings. The receptionist is soft of voice and wears clothes which combine a certain charm – the comfort of a nurse mixed with high street fashion. She talks so quietly

145

that I can barely hear her,

"Mrs. Kennedy, welcome to the clinic. Please take a seat".

I half expect her to hand me a room key, as the reception has a hotel foyer feel; lilies, glossy magazines, and brochures with discreet diagrams of the inner workings of the ovaries. I take a seat and wonder where Matthew is. He's been acting strange over the last few days. I thought he'd be happy to have financed his new deal. I shudder at the thought of Walsh and take a calming breath to remove his image from my memory. I've spent a lifetime removing bad images from my brain. I reassure myself that Matthew never breaks a deal and sit on my chintzy chair and wait for him to arrive. I try not to remind myself that every time I feel like something is going to work out, life comes along and decides that I am not due what I think I want. I have about five minutes of innocent hope left before I watch the hands of the clock tick past my allocated appointment time. And this is how it pans out. On the morning of our appointment, Matthew sends me a text. He breaks our deal.

I sit in a chintz covered armchair in Doctor God's fertility clinic's waiting room, reading lifestyle magazines. My Pilate's exercised, spray tanned legs are crossed and defensive. I look around at the other couples and notice that I am the only woman without a partner, leading to occasional glances from the other clients. They are probably assuming that I am a career woman who lives with a cat called Sheba and makes elaborate breakfasts

146

for the two of on Sundays, consisting of kippers and dairy products to bring warmth to my cold-hearted money-obsessed life. The eyes flicker back and forward to me. I ignore the receptionist's call of,

"Mrs. Kennedy, MRS KENNEDY (her voice raises slightly). We are ready for you now".

The chintz-choked room and the cut-glass vases of funereal lilies can't quite mask the stench of fear among the beautifully clad couples. I force myself to read Matthew's text.

-Can't make it, cot in important mtg-.

I wonder if the 'cot' is intentional? I don't press reply. Instead, I stand up, ignore the 'Mrs. Kennedy, Mrs. Kennedy' and become consumed with a white-hot nuclear energy that propels me two squares down to Matthew's glass-surround office. I stop off at the chichi office bistro on the ground floor. I take an empty coffee cup and lid from the counter. When the cashier asks for payment for the cup as I have left my handbag in the clinic, I take off a diamond bracelet and put it in the staff tips bucket. I ignore the nice girl saying,

"But missus, that is crazy".

I laugh a little in the manner of a Bond villain as I think, that is not crazy, wait till you see crazy, as I wait for the lift to descend. I get into the lift, face the stainless-steel panels, and use them as a temporary mirror to fix my hair and make-up. The lift pings and I arrive at the executive floor. The doors open and a scent of expensive scent hits my nostrils. Matthew's secretary sits straight-backed at a computer screen and swivels on her high-tech chair as she hears the lift open. She pastes a fake smile on her face when she sees me, dressed immaculately in my white trouser suit but ruining the look with crazed eyes.

"Oh, Angela, I don't think Matthew is expecting you", she says, and I look closely at her and realise she is blushing. Another Matthew love casualty, I mentally note.

"Let me just buzz through and I'll ask him to pop out", she continues, but I'm already opening the door.

She follows me to the door, peeks her head around and stutters slightly as she says,

"Oh God. I'm sorry, Matthew. I know you are in a meeting but…".

She's not sure what to do, poor girl. I almost feel sorry for her. Nothing in her executive personal assistant training manual would have prepared her for a furious wife with an empty coffee cup. I say gently to her,

"It's OK. He won't mind".

She returns to her desk, and I am left facing Matthew and the trio of men who were at my house the other night. I avoid their gaze and watch Matthew squirm slightly, a variety of looks fighting for supremacy. He settles on a genial husband look; a kind of Cary Grant exasperated with Doris Day's ditsy housekeeping skills. And a smattering of Ted Bundy.

"Angela. So lovely to see you, sweetheart. In town shopping?".

I cut him dead and say,

"You know why I'm in town, Matthew".

'Cary Grant' disappears as he walks around to where I stand and leads me to the cappuccino maker, where Walsh is standing. Matthew whispers into my ear,

"You look like a crazy woman. I'm trying to get some work

done here…"

Walsh smiles at me hesitantly and then gazes at his shiny tan brogues.

"I'll get you coffee. Fill up your cup, Angela. God, women, what are you supposed to do with them?", Matthew says, and the men laugh half-heartedly.

I hand Matthew the cup, just as Walsh stretches to reach it.

"Fill it, please!", I say, and I'm surprised to hear my voice sound so reasonable, almost Doris Day like in its chirpiness. This acting is addictive, I think. Walsh presses some buttons on the cappuccino maker, but Matthew and I know, eyes locked together, that coffee is not to be the beverage of choice this particular afternoon. Matthew turns to the businessmen and says,

"You know, guys, I think we are up to date here. Rain check?".

He ushers them through the door so fast that I only have a moment to ask Walsh how his wife is. He doesn't answer and moves as fast as he possibly can to get away from Matthew's office. I point to Matthew's cup and say,

"We had a deal, Matthew. Fill it, please".

He walks to his executive bathroom and fills my cup. I
water his plants. He arrives back into the office, hands me
the cup and starts to speak. I place my finger on his mouth.

"Text me", I say,

I get back into the lift, travel to the ground floor and walk
past the bistro girl who is now wearing the bracelet. She
attempts half-heartedly to take it off, but I say,

"Keep it. It suits you", and I make my return journey to the
clinic.

I arrive back in the clinic, hand the cup to the disgusted
receptionist, who disappears somewhere with it for testing,
I hope. I cross my legs, open one of the glossy magazines
and admire photographs of celebrities, arms wrapped
around each other in exotic locations and await my
appointment. Well done, Angela, I smile to myself. The
whale music has certainly made you calm and efficient this
lovely, sunny day.

CHAPTER 17

MATTHEW:

I've taken to sitting in Stephen's Green, admiring ducks. It certainly beats sitting in my office avoiding the non-stop phone calls. Belly up, market crash, investors screaming for my blood and those three horrible words from my accountant.

No. Further. Credit.

If I thought Angela turning up at my office was a fuck-up, well, that had nothing on how today has turned out. O' Dwyer rang me at 9 am, requesting we meet 'pronto'. I walked to the cafe around the corner, and he jumped up from his seat the moment he saw me and acted all KGB on me, until we found a quiet corner of the Green to sit in. He was wearing a black tie, like he was heading to a funeral. He looked rough, as if he had slept in his suit and his eyes looked like one of his kids had attacked him with a biro they were so dark-ringed.

"Stop looking at my eyes. I haven't fucking slept since I last saw you", he snapped, the two of us sitting there on a bench watching the park come to life, like pensioners.

"What's up, Brian?", I asked him, wanting this over and done with, so I could go back to sorting out my business.

He had his head down and was quiet and then I noticed that he was crying. Fucking crying like a two-year old. Big dirty tears were soaking his shirt. He didn't have to tell me. I knew. I could feel it in my bones for weeks.

"Everything's fucked", he eventually said.

"How bad?", I asked, determined to stay calm. Keep focused, Matthew, that's the only way.

He took one of those jagged breaths that kids take when they are wired and said,

"West Wharf has taken it all, Matthew. Your money is all tied up in that project. The deposits from interested buyers are minimal. So, although you own the land, well partly, you and your investors do, there are no cash deposits coming through so there is no money to develop it. Your portfolio is fucked too. All the values of the properties are plummeting, and the way things are going, I'd say you'll be in negative equity in a few months' time. Weeks, even".

I sat there and listened. And thought of all my lovely cranes on building sites all over Dublin. And noticed my phone buzzing – Hennessy, Walsh, O'Brien. Baying for my blood, their millions parked in a development that will never get built. And O' Dwyer sat there crying like a baby.

"I put money in West Wharf too, you know", he said.

"Boo fucking hoo", I said to him and that's when he tried to punch me. So, I had two options. I could sit there and face his wrath, the first time he risks his own money with me, and it flops, spectacularly.

"I don't force people to invest, Brian. I didn't hold a gun to your head and say, give me your millions".

"I'm going to lose my house", he said and then he started to cry again.

Or I could take the second option - run.

And that's what I did.

I ran. From the calls, from O' Dwyer, from everybody. And that's how I ended up on the other side of the park with a bottle of whiskey in a brown paper bag, looking at the ducks and laughing to myself.

Until the cop came up with a woman holding a toddler in her arms beside him, saying,

"I thought he looked a bit odd", an audience of nosey fucking parkers nodding their heads behind her.

And the cop says,

"Sir, it might be better if you go home".

He helped me up from the ground and I mustered every bit of dignity I had left, looking into his corn-fed country boy's face, and said,

"The sky is falling down".

The mother with the toddler made a screw-ball gesture at me. The nice young country guard led me away and put me into a taxi and sent me home. Well, home for the time being anyway. I've got to get rid of this overpriced mausoleum. And get out of here before they all come and get me. I arrive at my house for the first time ever during the week in daylight hours, switch on the T.V. and then promptly turn it all off again. The economic experts are everywhere. I think about what my mother says to me at least twice a year.

"One of these days, you'll get your comeuppance, Matthew Kennedy".

Her wish has finally come true. I have failed. Spectacularly. I am finished. Done. I could write a country and western song about it. It's that fucking tragic. I laugh till I nearly cry.

CHAPTER 18

MARTHA:

I always find the anticipation of a party is the best part of it. I decide to borrow a dress from Mum's wardrobe. Dad has cleared out some of her clothes, depositing bags to various charity shops around Dublin. This hasn't been an easy task for him, but despite my offer to help, he decided to do it on his own. "Gives me something to do", he said. The work on the mews is nearly finished and I am amazed at how transformed it is. Dad said he did plenty of manual work on building sites before his musical career became a paying one. This surprises me as I don't connect the delicacy of his piano playing with the raw, hard work of the building site. People have a habit of displacing your previous opinions of them, just when you think you know everything about them. I do have a very old memory of him covered in dust and dirt, pushing me on the swing in the garden under the apple tree, *higher, daddy, higher*, and him laughing as I felt I could fly right off that swing all the way out to Lambay Island. I stand in front of Mum's wardrobe, afraid to open it for some superstitious reason. I feel like an intruder in their bedroom, but Dad walks in and says,

"Go on, Martha, one of us needs to have some fun around here".

I kiss him on the forehead and grab him by the hand to help me choose. It's very fortunate that Mum and I are the same size – size ten, five foot seven- but for some reason she always seemed taller, something to do with a childhood filled with ballet, or charisma. Charisma tends to add inches to a person's height.

"OK, Martha, what's it to be?", Dad says, and I open the wardrobe tentatively, breathing deeply.

There is a faded scent of roses from the clothes, and I stick my head in amongst the dresses and whisper,

"Mum".

Dad is stoic and encourages me to choose a dress.

"She would not have wanted to get old and wear old lady's clothes", he says to me, "That's what I keep saying to myself anyway".

I blink back tears and reply,

"She would have grown old disgracefully anyway. She would have taken to wearing silk kimonos, skyscraper heels and bohemian hats to cover the grey hair that would dare to grow in her hair".

Dad laughs a dimmed laugh and says,

"We'll never know now".

I remove a blue cotton day dress from a hanger and decide that it's the one. I have a feeling I may be over-dressed for a staff party but decide to seize the day and go for it. I part ways with Dad and spend some time getting ready. I've never been one for make up or hair preparations as I've always been too comfortable in jeans and warm sweaters for long beach walks and shell-collecting. Occasionally, when I stayed with school friends, I joined in and surprised myself by liking what I saw in the mirror, but felt it was only achieved by the alchemy of the make-up boxes my friends worshipped so much. I was always so happy to return home to my comfortable clothes and my solitary beach ramblings. I brush my hair for a while in homage to Granny's rigid one hundred strokes rule and tie it up in some sort of semblance of a grown-up hairstyle. I paint my face, apply jewellery and a mist of perfume which I walk into, so I am not overpowered by it. I catch a quick look at myself and decide that I look OK for a twenty-two-year-old busy nurse who's suffered *a terrible loss* in the last year, as Martina in the canteen would put it. I walk to the kitchen where Dad is sipping coffee and drawing a plan for the mews garden, and he whistles like the builder he looks like today. I spin around and pretend to be a girl who cares what clothes do for her,

"Why thank you", I say, and stop spinning as I feel slightly nauseous. I steady myself on the back of a kitchen chair and Dad whispers,

"She'd be thrilled you are starting to get out again, Martha. This is no place for a young girl like you".

I blow him a kiss and reply,

"Where else would I be?".

He smiles at me and then laughs,

"You were nearly there, Martha. But I have to say it has a certain avant-garde look to it".

I look at my Converse trainers and laugh with him. I'm not quite ready for heels. You can take the girl from the beach, but her choice of footwear will always give the game away.

"Right. I'm off. Have a nice evening yourself. Maybe, pop down to the village, have a pint? After whatever Mary has left you for dinner".

I walk towards the oven and lift the lid on the dish Mary has left for him and say,

"Does Mary have a book called '50 strange things to do with mince', because it seems to turn up in all our dinners? I shouldn't give out but...".

Dad interrupts and says,

"Poor Mary, she means well. Cooking is not her strong point but look, she's been so good to us too, keeping the house going while we are like two ghosts wandering the halls".

I agree and say,

"I know. Look, enjoy your evening and I'll try to be a good girl".

Dad smiles as he knows that I've always been a good girl and the sensible one of the three of us. I gather my keys, jacket and handbag and walk to my trusty little car. I wave at Dad, who stands at the kitchen window and realise that he didn't answer my question about whether he'd walk to the village for a pint. I suppose he gets tired of answering 'no'. I sit in the car for a moment, watching the waves and wonder what Dad would make of my old habit of writing messages in bottles, returning to my life. When I was six, I spent a whole summer writing messages on tiny bits of paper, carefully folding them over so that they'd squeeze into bottles. The messages were always the same -hello, my name is Martha, I live in Ireland by the sea, pls write back to me-. I finally gave up on them when Mary complained of the bottle theft in her pantry, but somewhere in your heart you are always a six-year-old girl who believes in the magic of the ocean. I've started sending them again since Mum died. I buy the bottles myself, write notes on my best writing paper with an old fountain pen and just like when I was six, they are always the same message.

Dear Mum, I hope you are free from pain. I will always think of you. I hope you are singing with the angels. Love Martha xx.

She never replies.

I start the ignition of the car before I go down the usual route of sadness and as it's my first real party since last year, I choose some pop music. I open the window and drive to Conor's house, allowing the wind to free strands of my hair and sing out loud and risk the stares of other motorists at traffic lights. Seize the day, Martha! I'm about halfway up the driveway to the nursing home and close to

162

Conor's cottage, when I hear the music. I frown as I don't want Conor to get into trouble with Gerard but banish the thought because that is the old Martha talking and tonight, I am wearing makeup, have an almost perfectly intact hairstyle and I want to have some fun. I park my car in front of the cottage and wave to some of my colleagues as they walk into the party. They look completely different to their normal buttoned-up selves, dressed in bright colours and tottering on high heels. I join them as they walk in and feel the buzz of a good night as the pulse of the music lightens my heart. Tony is in charge of the music, and he is surrounded by a few of his previous conquests – the poor girls who have fallen for his slightly tainted charm. He is wearing a dark polo top, so all his carefully acquired muscles are on display. He has worn the tightest jeans I bet he could find, and I try to ignore his wolf whistle as he watches me entering the room.

"Jesus, Martha, I wouldn't recognise you. You are a total babe", he says as he embraces me in the middle of the makeshift dance floor in Conor's sitting room. I extricate myself from his sweaty grasp and say thanks very quietly, annoying myself for looking like I care that he thinks I'm a 'total babe'. I go in search of Conor, try the kitchen and the bedroom which is locked and walk outside to where I find him sitting on a stone step drinking a can of beer and smoking a cigarette.

"Hi", I say shyly, and he stands up so quickly that he knocks over his can of beer.

"Oh, hi Martha. You look…", he says, as he turns the can of beer the right way around and I'm hopeful he won't say 'total babe' when he finishes his sentence,

"…pretty in blue".

I sit down beside him, and he offers me a can of beer from the stash behind him. We sit quietly for a while, occasionally turning our heads around when the music changes and the crowd get louder.

"Tony's taste in music is exactly how I thought it would be", he remarks.

I smile and say,

"Gangsta rap and Take That", and we both laugh until we are interrupted by Tony himself, who arrives outside with Katya, his female pick of the night, who is glued to his side.

"Would you not come in and join the bleeding party?", he says, a slur in his words.

He smokes a cigarette and ignores Katya's complaints about it being too cold outside. He watches Conor and I to such an uncomfortable level, that I give in and say,

"C'mon, Conor, I've never seen you dance. Let's go join the partaaay".

We walk past Tony and Katya and ignore the way he wobbles from side to side, reeking of booze and it's still only ten o'clock. Conor drinks a lot tonight. He is jittery and nervous and although he acts like a regular party-goer, I sense he is uncomfortable. It doesn't help that Tony is being a complete asshole and makes constant jibes at him.

"About time you had a social life, Conor, huh? Must be strange having actual people in your gaff? Martha only feels sorry for you. She's probably only dancing with you for a bet".

Tony gets drunker and waves his arms around randomly to an Eminem track. So, it doesn't surprise me when he bangs roughly against the wall of photographs and dislodges the photograph of Conor's mother. It crashes to the ground and Conor becomes agitated. Tony picks up the photo and says,

"Who's she then, Conor? Your dead wife who you've buried under the rosebushes?".

He is thrilled with his own humour and laughs so much at his own joke that he doesn't realise that no-one else is joining him. Someone turns the music down and the party guests retire in little knots to various parts of the sitting room. Conor says in a quiet, firm voice,

"Put the photo down. Please".

Tony ignores him and traces his finger around the frame of the photo and says,

"And if I don't. What will you do, Conor?".

One minute Conor is standing quietly beside me awaiting the return of his precious photograph and the next minute, he is punching Tony hard on the mouth, drawing blood. Tony loses his cool completely, calls him every curse word he can think of and punches Conor repeatedly. Everyone watches quietly as they inflict damage on each other. Conor is in some kind of rage and Tony's drunkenness slows him down so that Conor is hurting him more. I snap out of my shocked silence and walk bravely towards them. Tony sees me out of the corner of a bloodied eye and says,

"Keep the fuck out of it, Martha. It's got nothing to do…",

but before he can finish Conor starts to punch him again and I stand between them, my back to Tony and say as quietly as I can,

"He's not worth it, Conor. He's doing it on purpose because he wants to get you in trouble".

With the mention of the word trouble, a lot of the staff leave the room as they are hard workers and value their jobs. Conor's eyes are wild. I touch him on his cheek and make him look at me directly in the eyes. Someone leads Tony away and while I can hear his cries,

"Fucking let me at him, I'm gonna kill him",

I feel Conor's body go completely limp and he is saying something. I bring him into the kitchen where some of the staff are playing cards and ignoring the fight. Conor sits down on the floor. I sit beside him and I can hear Gerard's voice in the background shouting.

"What the hell is going on in here?".

I block out the noise and listen to what Conor is saying.

"I offered to go in his place. Just one time. Please. But the man said no. He didn't like dark-haired boys anyway, he whispered in my ear, especially ones who stick their noses into people's business, like me. I used to sit on the top of the landing and watch him go on his trips with the man, his head down low as the car drove away. I never saw him much after that. He was always too busy. The light went out in his eyes, and I wanted to put some light back into them, so I decided one day to bring all the comics that I'd saved for him to cheer him up. So, when he was back one day, I left the comics on his bunk. He just tossed them on the bedroom floor, turned his head away to the wall and said, 'Go away Conor, comics are for babies'. That's the last time I spoke to him until the day…".

He is interrupted by Gerard walking in and saying, in a furious tone,

"Conor, you'd better sort this place out. We let you have it as a favour, and you know that. So, get rid of everyone and I want to see no repeat of this. Are you listening to me?".

Conor has his head down and doesn't reply to Gerard. I lead Gerard away and tell him I will clean it up and make sure it is all quiet and cleared up within the hour. He seems comforted by that. He leaves, his keys jangling as he walks back down the path. I walk with him, and he asks me,

"What's up with Conor? Keep an eye on him, Martha".

We watch Tony and the other party guests getting into cars and listen as they talk about going to the pub. Gerard waits until they leave and walks back up to the nursing home. I clean up with a few of the other nurses, put Conor's Mum's photo back on the wall and say thanks and goodnight to the people who have helped me. I walk back to Conor in the quiet kitchen, put my arms around him and say,

"Do you fancy a visit to the seaside?".

He smiles a sad smile and replies,

"Yes".

We leave the cottage and I'm glad that I only managed to drink half a can of beer as I drive Conor away from his cottage and his memories.

CHAPTER 19

ANGELA:

I'm sitting in a chair in Doctor Smith's office at the clinic. He has an impressive wall of framed degrees and certificates. He's running late. Apparently, he's very much in demand. There's a wall of thank you cards to my left, which I glanced at briefly but tore my eyes away from as I am too terrified to even dare hope that I too, could be the sender of one of those cards someday. I specifically refuse to look at the snapshots of the babies on the wall to the right of me. I gave up all religion years ago but find myself praying today. I've never found anyone listened before, so I'll hold my opinion on all things religious, for the time being. Doctor Smith arrives, and my right leg starts to tremble, as it always does when I'm nervous. He has kind eyes, Doctor Smith, but something in the way he moves very rigidly makes me feel a little awkward with him. He is beautifully turned out and I have an image of a devoted wife ironing his ties while he is out making babies for us sad cases. I bet he has dozens of children who look like him, all neat and pressed crammed into a Victorian redbrick somewhere. I fantasise a lot about other people's lives. Someday I'll work it out. The how to be a family bit. I find myself thinking more and more of my own mother lately and wish that she was here today, to hold my hand and whisper in my ear that everything is going to be OK.

you get yourself into that room and you do what you are told, d'ya hear me, Angela? Or do you want me to call the Social? She's not coming back, you know that. Don't you? In your stupid, little head, you must know that. Go now, before he changes his mind and kicks you onto the street.

"Are we ready to start, Mrs. Kennedy? Mrs. Kennedy?", Doctor Smith interrupts my reverie.

I banish the voice in my head, sit up straight smile and say,

"Yes, apologies. Yes. Thank you".

Doctor Smith opens a brown folder on his desk, puts his reading glasses on, looks at me and asks,

"Your partner? Is he going to be here today?".

"Emm...not sure. He's a very busy man. Runs his own

property investment company".

Doctor Smith removes his glasses for a moment, smiles a cynical smile and says,

"Property investor? Well, I hope he has protected you, my dear. I believe it's all going to crash around our ears, if we are to believe what we read in the papers".

Matthew has been acting erratically for the last few weeks and I've taken to keeping a close eye on our joint finances. A beginner's guide to computing course I did to fill in the morning hours, years ago, is starting to pay off for me as I log online each day when he leaves and see cash disappearing in large sums.

"Does he need to be here for the results of the tests?", I ask, annoyed at the thought of any delay in finding out the results of all those invasive tests.

"Could we maybe phone him and get his permission?".

I try and hide my annoyance and smile sweetly at Doctor Smith. He makes a 'hmmph' sound, looks at his watch and replies,

"Technically, he should be here. If you make it quick, I'm

sure it will be OK".

I don't wait for him to change his mind and phone Matthew's phone number quickly, praying it doesn't go to voice mail.

"Yeah, Angela? What is it?", he replies, the sound of traffic muting him slightly.

"Matthew, you were supposed to be here today?".

"Where?".

I see Doctor Smith look at his watch again and I say to Matthew,

"Listen, it's OK. You just need to talk to Doctor Smith really quickly and give him your permission so he can give me all the results of the tests".

Matthew replies distractedly,

"Results? Oh, for fucks sake, not that as well. Angela, do you have any idea what's going on? I'm stressed up to my eyeballs…".

I stand up and walk to the wall of thank-you cards and interrupt him in a calm voice,

"Matthew, just say yes to the results, that's all you need to do. A minute out of your day. That's all".

There is a brief pause on the other end of the phone and a very subdued Matthew replies,

"OK, pass me over to him. And, Angela, just remember I love you.".

I'm confused by what he is saying but grab any lifeline and pass the phone to Doctor Smith. I watch the hands of the clock while they speak and in half a minute their conversation is over. Doctor Smith mutters something about this all being rather unconventional but opens my file anyway.

"OK, well first of all, the tests have all come back in. You are in excellent condition, Mrs. Kennedy".

He looks over at me as he says this and I suddenly have

sympathy for cattle on market day.

"Thanks", I reply, meekly.

Doctor Smith continues,

"Your womb and indeed all your reproductive organs are in great condition for a woman your age".

He holds an x-ray of an internal piece of me which I really would prefer not to think about, up to the light.

"Yes, great condition. Congratulations".

I reply,

"Thank you. There really should be a Hallmark card for that. Congratulations, your womb is in fantastic shape", and even while I'm saying this, I tell myself to shut up. Doctor Smith ignores me anyway. He has moved onto another page and peers very closely at it.

"Your husband? He's a young man?", he asks me.

"Forty-two this year. But he's active, goes to the gym and

doesn't smoke or drink that much", I reply.

"Well, Mrs. Kennedy, there is no easy way to say this. Your husband's tests all came back and trust me, we recheck everything, just in case. He is infertile. The fact that the result is so conclusive makes me think that he may have had a childhood disease such as mumps, or that he, how shall I put this delicately, may possibly have had a vasectomy".

I don't remember getting into my car. I know I thanked Doctor Smith and I know I paid my bill and I know I opened my car and drove out of the clinic. I don't even allow my mind to start to process the possibility of what Matthew may or may not have done, until I am sitting in a suburban cul-de-sac, parked outside his parent's house. I am taking deep breaths and working up the courage to ask Clare if Matthew had mumps as a child and hoping for his sake that he did. I walk up the path, admire the manicured lawn as I do and the window baskets, which are a riot of mauve and pink. I ring the doorbell and realise that I am nervous as the gentle bells echo somewhere in the pristine hall I can see through the shining glass. I have never been here on my own before in the twenty years that I've been with Matthew. We tend to see each other on perfectly orchestrated occasions, surrounded by work colleagues or in Clare's case, her lady friends from all her various hobbies and good works. She is a busy lady, is Clare and I wonder if it would have been different if I had children to present to her, if we could have forged some kind of friendship. Shared genes can produce miracles. Clare walks up to the hall door, looks suspiciously at me, checks herself, smiles benevolently at me, wipes her hands on her apron (flour, she's been baking) and opens the door.

"Angela, what a surprise. You didn't need to ring the doorbell. My God, you're not a stranger. Everyone else just pops around the side passage and sticks their heads into the kitchen".

We look at each for a second, both knowing that I am not a pop her head into kitchens type of daughter-in-law. I wonder briefly how much Matthew has told her about my past but decide to concentrate on the matter in hand.

"I hope I haven't disturbed you, Clare? Maybe I should have phoned ahead", I say, attempting a sweet and light daughterly tone.

Clare's oven timer bleeps in the background and she turns to walk to the kitchen saying,

"Angela, you don't need to phone ahead. Come on through to the kitchen. I'm baking scones for James's fund-raising drive. It's the least I can do".

I walk with her and two minutes later, she has a plate of scones, some home-made jam (from Derek's blackberry bushes) and a pot of English tea in a pot she made in pottery class (a woman's got to fill her time, Angela) in front of me. She sits down opposite me, and I look at all the photographs of her family on the wall facing me; Matthew and his brother, James; fishing, camping, holding trophies aloft in muddy rugby jerseys and say,

"I envy you, Clare, do you know that?".

Clare pours me tea and looks surprised.

"You envy me, Angela? I would have thought that you have such a fantastic life with Matthew that you would never envy anyone. All that travel and clothes and freedom, God, it's so different from my life".

She walks to the fridge to fetch cream and I'm vaguely wondering if she has her own cows to produce it, when she startles me by saying,

"He's always been a difficult one".

I sip my tea and say,

"Who? Matthew?".

"Yes, from the day he was born, he demanded every moment of my attention. A greedy little boy, grabbing

178

James's toys, from the moment he came into the world, nothing was ever enough for him. God, I sound disloyal. A mother shouldn't criticise her own son and I love him, but let's just say I know he hasn't been that fair to you".

I'm dumbfounded because Clare and I never get beyond talking about the weather or what work she is getting done in her house, so I'm surprised she's being so kind to me.

"Angela, take a look at this".

She takes me by the arm, and I follow her to the sitting room where she walks behind the door. There's a piece of wall that doesn't match the cool grey tone which the rest of the room is decorated in. I look closely and see different shades of paint and numerous patterns of wallpaper in the corner of the wall. Clare says quietly,

"Don't let it be you, Angela. All I do is re-decorate this house, every couple of years, paint charts and wallpaper samples. Forty years of it. Filling in the days, watching the world from my gorgeous house".

She reaches towards me and looks straight at me,

"I used to be an air hostess, did you know that Angela? I loved my job but decided that being a full-time mother and wife would be enough for me".

She looks out of the window as if she's trying to will an airplane to take her away and I ask her,

"But you raised two sons, Clare. You've got to give yourself some credit".

She interrupts me and walks back to the wall where she can view her forty years of decorating and says,

"They grow up, Angela. Then, you never see them. Look, I understand. They're busy, they've got work and wives and in James's case, whole villages of people to worry about. I am proud of them, but you know, sometimes I wonder, if only….".

Derek walks in then, carrying newspapers and enquiring if there are any scones left and Clare reverts to the old hostess that I know so well. Derek sits with us at the kitchen table for a while discussing the financial market and sounding a little smug when he says his money is all tied up safely. He asks,

"Rumour has it in the golf-club that Matthew is suffering? But I'm sure we are the last people he will tell. Matthew never likes to lose at anything".

He kisses me on the cheek and decides to tend to his prizewinning roses and before he leaves, he says,

"Just tell him he can come to us, Angela. We won't judge him. That's what family are for".

I thank him and help Clare load the dishwasher.

"He's lost it all, hasn't he, Angela?", she asks.

"I think he was over-ambitious, Clare. You know what he's like", I reply.

Her phone pings with a text message and she says,

"That's James. They are struggling to find finance for his new project in Africa. God, I can't remember the name of the place now. I have been helping him fund-raise but if they are to get the school and hospital built, they still need quite a lot of money. Guess, I'll just keep having to bake".

I ask her,

"Do you have a website address for his project, Clare? I'd like to help".

She finds a piece of paper and writes down the name of it and I place it in my handbag. Clare sits down at the table with me again. I ask her the question I came here to ask.

"Did Matthew ever have any childhood illness which might have caused problems, Clare? How shall I put it? Male issues?". She hesitates for a second and then says,

"You mean like mumps?".

"Yes", I say quietly.

"You know. I've always wondered why you two never had children. I've often said to Derek that you both probably didn't want babies as they'd interfere with your lifestyle. Or destroy your lovely figure, Angela. But now, I'm not saying anything, but I should have guessed there were maybe medical issues?".

I nod my head and just wish she would answer my question.

"Let me think. Now he had chickenpox. I remember that well, the two of them miserable and itching day and night.

182

And tonsillitis."

Hurry up. Clare. Answer it.

"And chest infections and sore throats. But mumps? Let me think".

I tap my nails on the table. Tip. Tap. Tip. Tap.

"No. Angela. Matthew never had mumps".

I smile falsely at her and leave. I drive to the only home I've had since Lizzy died, look at it in the evening sun and know without a doubt that I am going to be leaving it soon. Very soon.

CHAPTER 20

MARTHA:

I'm woken by the sound of seabirds, a familiar sound, but they sound closer today somehow. My nostrils are filled with the scent of coffee and paint. I remember I am in the mews, which is about one hundred yards from my home, stretch my legs and admire the cool mint colour Dad has applied to the walls of the bedroom. It's unrecognisable. He has de-chintzed the entire house, if that's possible and it barely holds any resemblance to how it was in Granny's hey-day. Granny was fond of parrots in cages, lace headrests, nests of tables and china pots of indoor plants everywhere. I leave my room and dress in last night's clothes. The blue dress looks a little less glamorous than it did last night. I walk into the bathroom and my senses are rewarded with a New England type palette of colours – white wood, pale blue walls and driftwood placed on the deep windowsill. I wash my face and run my hands through my hair, trying to avoid the panda affect which the dried-in makeup has inflicted on my eyes. I follow the scent of coffee, find the front door open and stop for a second when I hear the hushed sound of two male voices.

"Morning, Martha, you look, well, interesting, is the word that comes to mind", my father says, rising from his chair on the deck where he sits with Conor.

Conor looks around, sees me and smiles. I kiss them both and join them on the deck.

"Conor tells me you both had a bit of drama last night", Dad says, as he walks to the kitchen.

"Emmm. Yeah. Tony was being his usual self. Things got out of hand, you could say".

"I was just popping down to stain the deck when I came across Conor. Look, there's no rush. Stay all day, you two, if you like".

He continues walking to the kitchen and I hear the coffee machine operating again.

"Martha, I really should get going, you know", Conor says, and he stands up and looks out to sea.

"It's so peaceful here", he says, just as a rowdy flock of seagulls swoop down to inspect the crumbs on his plate.

I laugh, pat the chair beside me and Conor sits back down.

"They remind me of Tony's crew at the party last night. God, he's such an idiot. He just can't get used to the idea that we are, you know, friends", I say,

Dad arrives back with more coffee, hands me a mug and says,

"Get that inside you, Martha. It'll put some life in you, I hope".

He looks to Conor and tells him,

"She's terrible in the mornings. She needs about a litre of coffee before she can even function as a vaguely normal human being. Have you been seeing each other for long?", he asks. I hesitate slightly and say,

"I wouldn't say we are seeing each other exactly, but you know, we are friends, maybe more, maybe it's something. Oh, God, pour me more coffee. Dad, I'm embarrassing Conor".

Conor and Dad laugh, and I notice that they seem to have formed a quick friendship. I'd even go as far as saying they are allies, the way they look at me and laugh at my morning bedhead. It's good to hear Dad laugh, even if it is my lack of dignity that has been used to unite the two of them. Dad stands up and says with laughter in his voice,

"Don't mind me. I know when I'm being a gooseberry. Conor told me that he has never made sandcastles, Martha. Isn't that the most shocking thing you've ever heard?".

"Jesus. That is more than shocking. It is tragic", I reply.

"Yes, he said that the kids from St Jude's sometimes took trips to the seaside but for one reason or another, he never quite made it", Dad says and I'm surprised at the mention of St. Jude's and how easily Dad came by the information from Conor. I sit down beside Conor and say quietly,

"Well, that is about to change".

187

"Hall cupboard, top shelf", Dad says,

"Come up for breakfast in the house when you are done. I'll treat you both to the full works".

He walks away and I take pleasure in the fact that he is returning to one of the weekly rituals he used to have before Mum's death - a large breakfast waiting on the kitchen table for Mum and me on Sunday mornings after we had finished swimming.

"Fried bread? Two fried eggs each?", I shout after him and he laughs and shouts back,

"Of course. I promised the works and I meant it".

From behind me, Conor says,

"He seems great. Your dad?", and I reply,

"He is the best. When I was little, he used to bring me down here as soon as the sun rose. We'd tiptoe out of the house and Mary, the housekeeper, would have been charmed into making him a batch of fresh bread rolls. They'd sit under a tea towel in the pantry and Dad would scoop them into a bag, make a pot of coffee, grab some juice for me and we'd sneak out with our bounty for dawn sandcastle making".

"Sounds like Heaven, growing up here, the sea in front of you, two parents. It's about a million miles from what I had", Conor says.

I put my hand in his and say,

"Remember last night, when we came back here, and you mentioned Francis. Did something bad happen to him?".

Conor shuts down again. It's something I am getting used to as he doesn't like talking about the past and I let him off the hook.

"Come on, those sandcastles won't make themselves".

We walk towards the mews, and I continue,

"You are so lucky that you have never made sandcastles with anyone before. You are about to be tutored by the sandcastle Queen of Ireland. Be warned, I'm very competitive".

Conor walks with me, puts his hand out to reach mine and says,

"I'm not used to being close to people, Martha. No-one has ever tried to be my friend since Francis. I'd like us to be more than friends though. If that was possible, if you could put up with me, I mean".

I take his hand in mine and we stand there, lit by the morning sun and I smile and say,

"I think I might be able to put up with you, Conor. Just about".

He smiles then and I bring him to the house, check to see if Dad has managed to leave the buckets and spades in the usual storage place and I find them there. They are substantial metal spades and buckets for carrying sand or crustaceans in. I hand them to Conor to carry.

As I lift one of the buckets out, I hear the sound of glass being struck by the handle of one of them. I look into the back of the cupboard and find two of the bottles I sent the messages to Mum in the sea. I take them out, explain my innocent idea to Conor and open the bottles. Dad must have found them in a rock pool and fished them out. They are washed clean, and I can just about read the water-washed notes. I show Conor the note.

Dear Mum, I hope you are free from pain. I will always think of you. I hope you are singing with the angels. Love Martha xx-.

He kisses me on the cheek and just when I attempt to put my note back into the bottle, he says,

"There is something written on the back of it. Look".

I open the note again, spread it on the counter and there on the back of it, in Dad's writing, is a note from him,

I know it's not the same but know that I am here for you. Love Dad x.

The sun shines through the window and it prompts a resistance in me, a need to push the thoughts of death away, to just feel the warmth of dawn sand under my fingernails and become child-like and lost in the moment.

I put the note in my pocket and dare Conor,

"C'mon, sandcastle construction class commences in twenty seconds".

Conor joins in and we race down the sandy path where the sea glistens with the first rays of sunlight. As we run, we kick off our shoes and I think of nothing else but the height of the castle I am about to build. We spend an hour constructing our pieces of beach architecture. Conor's castles bear a resemblance to the Leaning Tower of Pisa. I reassure him that they are very good for a beginner and as I watch him concentrate on his construction, I wonder how it could be that at the age of twenty-four, he has never had such a simple pleasure. I am completing my very last one when Dad appears beside us, blocking out the sun and saying that his feast of breakfast meats and sundry other items awaits us in the kitchen. Conor finishes his last sandcastle and Dad says,

"You are a natural, Conor".

Conor smiles and I walk between these two men, one from my past and one from my future and thank Mum wherever she is for sending Conor to me. I whisper to Dad as we get to the kitchen,

"Thanks for the note, Dad".

He looks bemused for a moment, wondering what I refer to. I inch the letter slightly out of my pocket, and he nods and says,

"We're getting there, Martha".

We sit in the kitchen, the three of us, lost in conversation about everything and nothing and eat the feast Dad has prepared. While we are there, our sandcastles are washed over by the incoming morning tide. Conor is a little upset when we stroll back to the beach and see this. Dad laughs and says to him,

"You'll just have to come back another day to make some more".

CHAPTER 21

ANGELA:

I walk into my house, close the front door, and lean against it. It's interesting how you can live a life, wake in the same bed beside the same man for twenty years and in a split second, you know it's over. Matthew and I have been acting out parts for most of our marriage. I suppose you could say we didn't have the best of beginnings. The past is starting to swirl around inside my head. The memories which I'd locked away and discarded are back with a vengeance. 1988 is running on a loop in my mind.

City centre hotel. I'm wearing a cheap short skirt. It feels itchy against my thighs. The girls I'm with are bitchy and blue. It's a slow night and only one girl has managed to pick up some business. Snow White we call her because she looks like the Fairy Tale princess with dark hair, clear blue eyes, and pale, translucent skin. She has a breathless, almost child-like voice which the customers love to listen to. Each to their own. I tell the girls to keep their voices down. We don't want to draw attention to ourselves and get flung out on the street by the bouncers. Mostly, they turn a blind eye. Liam, the man who in a leap of imagination, we call our manager, must be giving them a share of the takings. No-one does anything in this world unless there's a wad of cash pressed into their hands.

I run my fingers through my newly dyed blond hair. I'm wearing pink lip gloss and have to remember to smile every so often as Liam says I affect business with my scowl. I wear a tight pink top which shows off a few inches of bare midriff. Young skin is a currency here. Arthur spotted my potential a good few years ago. "She needs to earn her keep, Anna", I heard him say through the plaster wall in Anna's flat. Anna hesitated, but not for long enough, if you asked me at the time, but then nobody asked me anything because I was the girl with the dead, alcoholic mother. I had stopped turning up at school when they asked me too many questions.

"How's your mother, Angela? You're living with your aunt? Why have you got bruises on your legs?". I didn't want to go into the system because I'd seen what the system did to

girls like me with dead mothers. I thought I was safe with Anna, Lizzy's best friend. But Anna was in love with Arthur – small time criminal and pimp. I prayed hard the first night he brought a 'man-friend' to visit me. "Beautiful young girl like you, Angela, you should be sharing what God gave you, with other men", the first one said. I blocked out everything about him- the hair coming out of his ears, the smell of Rothmans and cheap whiskey combined on his breath. I concentrated on the damp stain on the wall which I imagined was a map of the world. Lucy and I planned to get out of there and travel the world and find two perfect gentlemen to marry us. The first time was over in about three minutes. I turned my face to the wall and ignored the pound notes on my bedside table.

Anna came in with a towel and a change of clothes, but I ignored her. She was muttering to herself and saying, "sure what choice did I have, Angela, he'll only bring good clean men to you, I promise". The men continued until Anna and Arthur had enough for a bolt hole in Malaga. Anna sat flicking through a brochure one morning, "Imagine, Angela, sunshine all day and I can pick oranges off a tree. I'm not sure if I'll go for the one that has a separate dining area or the one with the wrap-around balcony", she said.

Fuck off and die, Anna, I wanted to say, but instead I gave her a polite smile and said, "Go with the wrap-around balcony". "She's an odd one, Arthur", Anna said, when Arthur joined her to leaf through brochures of villas purchased from stolen flesh. He lit up the room when he came in. Matthew. With a group of men with sharp suits and confidence. I stood there in the foyer of the hotel, trying to quieten the two girls down as they kept squabbling. I heard his voice. Knew it already, in my head, I guess. "She's an odd one, Arthur"- maybe Anna was right. Matthew stopped dead in front of me and it could have been like a Hollywood movie moment. It was something at first sight. Love might be stretching it a bit. He was twenty-one , dark-haired and there was something about him that drew me to him. He said, "Can I buy you a drink?". His friends laughed, wondering what Matthew was doing with a bargain basement prostitute when he could have had anyone he wanted without cash changing hands. But Matthew never does what's expected of him. I stepped towards him. Placed my hand in his and said, "Glass of white wine, thanks", and that was it. There wasn't a bolt of lightning. There was just a connection between a girl in a cheap skirt with a desire to erase her own life and enter someone else's.

I take a deep breath and focus on my breathing. I admire

the beautiful hall, decorated by someone else in gold and buttermilk shades. The designer took one whole day to choose the buttermilk colour on a paint chart. I walk around the downstairs rooms where all the curtains are drawn, and the only sound comes from expensive clocks ticking in the reception rooms. It is like a stage set, awaiting characters to burst into action and bring the house to life. But no-one walks in from the wings. I text Lucy.

-escape from Alcatraz in motion-.

She replies,

-You sure, hon? -

-one thousand per cent- I reply.

-opening wine. See u whenever suits you - she texts back.

I switch off my phone and sit at my desk. I spend a little while moving a few hundred thousand Euro around accounts from places Matthew doesn't know I have access to. Sorry, sweetheart, I think, the few hundred thousand won't help you now. I log off the computer, look at my books and decide to take just one, the Greek myths volume, as it's become a favourite by now in the Angela academy of self-education. I walk up the stairs to my secret nursery and it's there I almost become undone. I am the queen of self-convincing by now and I start thinking once again that Matthew will come around and that he'll love a baby when he sees it. This is a train of thought which I've grown used to over the past five years, since we've been officially trying. Matthew is infertile, Angela. That thought mobilises me. I move the muslin-draped cot to one side, remove the already loosened floorboards and gather my collection of escape items; jewellery Matthew gave me on special occasions, forgotten by him the moment it was admired by an audience. Diamonds and rubies should be easy to trade for cash. I find the envelopes of cash that I've filled with regular trips to the ATM.

"Jesus, Angela, you spend a lot of money on housekeeping",

Matthew says so often that it's a game now, as he loves the idea of a florist arriving with half a van load of flowers for dinner parties hosted by him. Most of the time they were chain store bunches, arranged with a bit of random flair by me. The savings I've made in my housekeeping would make a war-time wife almost proud. All the wads of cash now sit in envelopes beneath the cot. And in Lucy's attic. I walk to the wardrobe and find a gym-bag. I load it with my getaway stash and walk to my bedroom. It's still dark in here from this morning when I left to find out my fate at the fertility clinic. I look at myself in the mirror, the fake middle-class housewife with an empty womb. I look at my hair, almost girlish in its length. I look at the expensive make up, the flawless skin. I don't like the Angela in my reflection. I'm tired of being her. I change my clothes first.

Remove the trouser suit and the heels. I erase the old Angela. It takes only minutes. I dress in black Lycra, remove my make up (You are worth it, Angela) and cut my hair as well as I can into a sharp bob. I've always loved the edges of those short sharp bobs with razor cut edges that could harm a person with their precision. I smile as I see the new version of myself in the mirror. I definitely prefer her. I pack a few items in a suitcase, search for my box with all my belongings from the flat I shared with Lizzy and smile when I see the familiar face of the señorita with the fan outstretched in her hand.

"Time to leave, Señorita", I say out loud and that's when Matthew arrives.

"Talking to dolls now, Ange?", he says, walking towards me and I realise that he has been drinking as he slurs his words.

I stand in front of the mirror tidying my hair with the scissors.

"A woman's got to have someone to talk to around here, Matthew. The silence could drive you nuts".

He sits on the bed and watches me.

"What's with the hair? Off to join a convent or something?".

"I just decided to do a little snipping of my own", I reply in a kind of sing-song voice that doesn't really sound like my own. To my own ears, it sounds a little Kathy Bates like from the movie, Misery.

"You dirty birdy, Matthew", I whisper.

He's too out of it to notice and closes his eyes as he lies on the bed, his legs and arms outstretched as if he awaits a crucifixion. His voice is husky as he says,

"It's all gone. I'm fucked. I need to work out my next step, Angela. You need to stop this baby shit and start acting like my wife".

I turn to him with the scissors in my hand.

"Matthew, when did you have a vasectomy?", I ask.

He sits up abruptly with no look of remorse on his face.

"I've never had a vasectomy. You're imagining…".

I stand over him with the scissors in my hands and point it vaguely at him. He reaches out for it, his hand on mine and we wrestle with it until Matthew's strength wins and the force of the struggle makes him awkward, and the scissors cuts his arm. There's a spot of blood on his white shirt, like he's been shot, and he is annoyed.

"For fuck's sake, Angela. That shirt was expensive".

He grabs a tissue from a box on the bedside table and wipes his self-inflicted wound.

"OK. Five years ago. I was supposed to be in Croatia, looking at some hotels. I had the procedure then".

I stand beside the bed and say quietly,

"You bastard".

I walk away then, taking my bag with me. Matthew follows me down the stairs.

"Where the fuck are you going?".

I don't turn around as I say,

"Anywhere but here".

We stand in the hall, the two of us slightly out of breath. Matthew becomes contrite and puts his arms around me.

"You can't leave me, Angela. I've lost everything. You can't leave me here on my own".

I step away from him. He's almost whining. And Matthew never whines.

"Why did you let me do it, Matthew? Encourage me to flirt with your colleagues. Sleep with some of them in the early days. Crappy sex and blackmail! You treated me like a slave, to use as you wished. You were no better than Arthur".

Matthew is incensed as he doesn't like to be compared to an inner-city pimp.

"You got a great life, Angela. Slave, you're kidding me. Slaves don't have fucking five-star hotel breaks every month. You would have been dead in a few years if I hadn't rescued you from that hotel. OK, some of the stuff we both did in the early years was out of order. But look around you, this is all ours".

We look around the hallway and the anger deserts me.

"It's all yours, Matthew. I can't do it anymore. The act. I'm not good at this life".

I walk towards the front door, carrying my baggage awkwardly. Matthew's whining goes up a gear.

"Angela, I love you. You know that. I never wanted kids. They would have fucked it all up. This life. Parties and weekends away. I've seen what it does to other people. They get old when they have kids. It's just not for me".

I turn around and shout into his ear,

"You could have told me".

I take a deep breath to calm down, think of all the pregnancy tests I have bought over the last five years and the fact that there was never going to be a blue line. Matthew knew that. He steps away from me and talks quietly.

"I'm sorry, Angela. About all of it. But don't go. We can talk.

Negotiate".

"I'm not one of your businessmen, Matthew. Negotiate. For fuck's sake. I'm gone. Can I ask you one question? Did you ever love me?".

Matthew smiles sadly and says,

"I did and still do. I wanted to rescue you from that hotel the moment I saw you. You were so beautiful and so fragile".

I walk up to him, touch him on the cheek and kiss him one last time.

"Rapunzel is all grown up now, Matthew. I can take it from here myself".

He starts to talk. I walk to the cleaner's Mini, open it and pack my belongings in the boot. I drive out of Tudor Drive until Matthew is just a small dot in the wing mirror. It's around six when I arrive at Lucy's. I take one of the boxes out of the boot and look through it. I sit outside Lucy's house for a while, hesitant to bring myself and my sorry load of possessions into her house. Lucy has a clean life and I'm not ready to pollute her with my issues yet. I sit for a while, listening to the radio and let the babble of an over-excited D.J wash over me. After a while, the passenger door opens, and Lucy sits in the seat. She kisses me on the cheek and says,

"You alright, Ange? Was Matthew fuming?".

I close my eyes, lean against the seat, and say,

"He had a vasectomy, Luce. Strung me along for the last five years. All those tests, not being pregnant, every single month and the fertility clinic. It was all a waste of time".

Lucy surprises me as I was expecting a 'he is a bastard' rant from her.

"Maybe you are better off without him, Angela. You never made each other happy anyway. You were both addicted to each other. It wasn't healthy".

I sigh and say,

"Maybe you're right, but I got used to him. It was good sometimes. You are so lucky to have escaped Arthur".

Lucy is sad and replies,

"I feel so guilty, Angela. I kind of knew what was going on in your flat, but I just didn't know what to do to make it better".

"I know, Lucy. But you were just a teenage girl yourself and we had no power at all. Your mother saved you".

Lucy raises an eyebrow and says,

"The typing course. I remember. "Go and learn how to type, Lucy. Get a job in an office", she said. I wanted to be a film star or a singer back then. I thought my mother was insulting my future brilliance by making me sit in that stupid typing class for two months, cursing that typewriter with its wonky keys".

I laugh and say,

"It got you out of there. You started wearing skirts and blouses and I was so proud of you, Luce. I remember seeing you walk past my window one morning and you were going to your first job and I thought, do it, Lucy, for both of us. I was still recovering, and I felt sad and lonely, but there you were, heading off to type your way out of those flats".

Lucy touches my hand and says,

"I'm so sorry, Angela. We didn't want you going back to Anna's flat after those few horrible weeks. And then, you went and got involved with Liam, the toe rag. I just couldn't figure you out and there was no stopping you. You were always a stubborn cow".

I smile and say,

"I know, Luce. My head was so screwed up and I didn't want to bring you down with me. You had your life, and you know what, when you started going out to do your typing course, it was the opposite. It didn't make me feel worse. It gave me hope".

Lucy smiles sadly and says,

"Do you remember when we used to sit on the swings and pretend we were going to fly up into the air and travel over to London to marry Wham?".

I laugh and reply,

"Yes. You wanted to marry Andrew Ridgely and I wanted to be Mrs. George Michael. Even then, I should have known I was always going to pick the wrong man".

We laugh, Lucy and I and she says,

"I see you still have Señorita. I used to think she was so sophisticated. Remember when Lizzy used to dance her little Spanish dance to imitate her?. God, I loved Lizzy almost as much as you did Angela. Poor Lizzy".

We both look at Señorita, her chin still tilted in that proud way, her dress a bit scruffy and tarnished from all the years of carrying her around. I take a bundle of cards out of the box and hand them to Lucy. She takes them out, starting with the one with the blue teddy bear,

"For a special boy who is 1 today", on the front of it. She reads them all and sighs when she reads the very last one which has a picture of a cartoon boy kicking a football into a net.

Have a special day, now you are 12.

Lucy is tearful as she reads my messages on the cards. They all end with the same line, 'love and kisses from your mam'.

"You never sent them?", she says.

"I never knew where he was. By the time I knew anything about him, it was too late".

Lucy packs all the cards back into the box, closes it and says,

"You never talk about the past, Angela. Any time I ever brought it up, you just clammed up. So I got to the stage when I just didn't mention it again. Come on, let's get you inside and pour us both a large glass of wine. I'd say you could do with one, after dealing with Matthew. What did he say?".

I grab my handbag and get ready to go into Lucy's house and reply,

"He wanted to negotiate with me".

Lucy starts to laugh and says,

"I shouldn't laugh. But that is so typical of Matthew, like you are a customer with a business problem".

"I'll fill you in on it all when we are having our wine. Remember you said she was back?".

"Anna?", Lucy replies.

"Yeah".

"I think I might be nearly ready to see her. There's stuff I need to find out".

Lucy pats my hand and says,

"Good. But for now, I'm getting you settled. Tonight is about getting you a couple of glasses of wine and a good night's kip".

"Thanks, Luce", I whisper as we walk into the house together. Lucy puts on a bright smile and shouts into the house,

"Look who's come to stay. Only Aunty Angela".

Dave comes to the door, carrying Jason in his arms and Amy smiles when she sees me. Dave says,

"We are delighted to have you, Ange. Welcome to the mad house".

Lucy closes the front door and I exhale for what feels like the first time in months.

CHAPTER 22

ANNA:

I'm packing up my handbag with bits and pieces – hospital appointment card, water, silvermints, lipstick (who am I kidding?), when there's a knock at the door. It's probably those young fellas again. The problem is they think it's a game that hasn't been played for years but they still do it anyway. Knock on the door, aul wan like me shuffles out to open it and they laugh their heads off as they tear off down the stairs, while I stand there looking like an eejit. I only open the door because I'm a stupid old woman who still believes in romance and thinks one of these days it will be Arthur at the door coming to mind me. He'll be standing there with his goofy smile and a large bunch of roses in his hands for me. They are probably right about the medicines I'm taking, as delusional is exactly what I am if I think that's every going to happen. I snap my handbag closed, take a very fast look in the mirror before the full horror of how I look hits. Not too bad for a near dead woman, I think, and the doorbell rings again. Jesus, I thought they had lots of stuff to amuse themselves with these days; computer games and online bullying or whatever they find to fill their time with. I peek through the net curtain and notice it's yellowing which is not like me as I have always been very house-proud but have dropped my standards since I've no Arthur to impress. Anyway, cancer has interfered with my housekeeping skills. It takes all my energy just to deal with it every day. I see a familiar face outside my flat and she looks very determined to stand there ringing my doorbell all day if she has to, so I let her in.

"Anna, you look…em…shit".

I gesture for her to come in and say,

"Lucy, thanks for the compliment. I certainly have seen better days".

I tidy my hair self-consciously and notice Lucy is staring at the bald patches. She, however, looks the picture of health, glowing with vitality; eyes clear, hair glossy and a look on her face that would strike you dead.

"Right, I'm prepared to put up with you being here, Anna, if you promise to get some answers for Angela", she says, a look on her face as if she can't bear the sight of me. I interrupt her.

"I've nothing to say to Angela. It's all in the past now, Lucy. You should just leave it alone. Nothing good will come from it now".

Lucy moves fast and before I know it, she stands right in front of me, her breath on my face as she says,

"You don't get to decide this. You've done enough harm. This is about Angela now".

I back away from her quickly, my heart palpitating and reply,

"I don't know why you want to dredge it all up, Lucy. I thought Angela was married to some big shot businessman now. You see, it all worked out for her in the end. She must have a few kids by now".

I walk to the door and gesture for Lucy to leave.

"I've got a hospital appointment in an hour. You'd better leave. I haven't got time for this".

Lucy walks outside with me and just as I think she is giving in easily, the taxi I ordered pulls into the car park below. The taxi driver honks the horn and Lucy says,

"Grand. I'll come with you. Keep you company, so to speak".

She's wearing that cheeky look she's had since she was a girl and I say,

"Don't be so stupid, Lucy. You can't come to the hospital with me. I'll be there for hours".

We walk down the stairs in silence and out to the car park. I get into the back seat and Lucy opens the other passenger door and brazen as anything, gets in beside me. The minute the car pulls out onto the road, she starts asking questions.

"Where did you bring him, Anna?". "What was his name?". "Where is he buried?".

I am so exhausted from her that by the time we get to the hospital, I budge a bit and tell her,

"Bring Angela to me. Or I can meet you somewhere? I really don't know what I can do to help".

She leans into me and says,

"What's wrong with you, Anna?".

"Cancer", I reply, and the taxi driver smiles at me, sympathetically, in the mirror.

Lucy takes a deep breath and says,

"I shouldn't really feel sorry for you, Anna, but you know, I am a decent human being unlike you. Cancer is a horrible thing to get, even for someone like you".

I laugh a bit and she says,

"Why are you laughing, Anna? You really are a mad old witch".

I reply,

"I'm laughing because you haven't changed one bit, Lucy. Still Angela's best friend, fighting her corner and looking out for her. She's lucky to have you".

She surprises me by becoming tearful and says,

"Well, somebody had to look after her. You let her down. You betrayed her completely. For that gobshite, Arthur. I hope he was worth it. Mind you, Mam says there's no sign of him around. Stayed in Spain, did he? Little weasel, just when you need him. Afraid he'd get arrested. Not nice to be left on your own, is it, Anna? I've always said what goes around comes around".

She gets out of the taxi. I pay the taxi driver and he asks,

"Are you alright, love? She's a bit much, especially for someone in your delicate condition".

"She's saying nothing I don't deserve", I reply and I give him a big tip as someone may as well have a good start to their day. Lucy writes down her phone number on a piece of paper, hands it to me and says,

"Ring me soon, OK. Angela needs answers. Emm…how

bad is it? Your cancer?".

"Not long now. A few months maybe".

She starts to walk away as I put her phone number in my handbag. She looks back and notices that I'm frail and can't walk very well. I have no dignity left and walk as carefully as I can, because if I walk too fast nowadays, I start to fell nauseous and then I have to sit down for a while. I'm not going to do any of that in front of Lucy, but even though I've worn ugly thick soled trainers today, my stilettos gathering dust in the back of my wardrobe, I still stumble slightly. As I'm steadying myself, a firm hand helps me up and she's there helping me, a martyred look on her face and says,

"Right, I won't be able to live with my conscience if I don't help you into your hospital appointment. C'mon, where is it? Just as long as you realise, I'm only helping you because I want you to make this appointment and do whatever they tell you to do, so you live long enough to get to meet Angela".

I catch a glimpse of the two of us as we take the lift-me, stooped, white-faced and almost bald with a granny dress on that I wouldn't have been seen dead in a few months ago and Lucy, curvy, lush with beautiful hair and skin. I look away from the reflection and we silently await the ping of the lift door as I head to my last appointment. Lucy nods goodbye and says that she'll be waiting for my call. I walk

away from her, willing myself to stand up straight and not
to tumble. I relax when I hear the lift doors close.

CHAPTER 23

MATTHEW:

I wake up on the floor of my home office, afraid to move my head because I know it's going to hurt like hell after drinking the best part of a bottle of whiskey. Note to self: it doesn't matter how expensive the whiskey is, you'll still wake up with the taste of death in your mouth and a headache which would almost admit you to hospital.

"Get up, Matthew", I say, loudly to myself.

It must be contagious, this talking to yourself. I'm becoming like Angela and the way she talks to her creepy old Spanish doll. I force myself to move and walk to the window, trying to figure out if it's still night-time or if I have moved onto another fascinating shit day in my life. It's starting to get light outside. I can hear traffic faintly in the background, all the good citizens heading off for another day of their work life, clocking in, clocking out. I have clocked out of my working life. I can't go near the office. There are way too many angry middle-aged men arriving to demand funds back. They think I have a magic wand and can go, abracadabra, there's your money back. The problem is that people don't read the small print. They are too greedily obsessed and drunk on how much cash my latest endeavour is going to make for them. Investments may go up or down, people, it says it there in the small print which you would need a magnifying glass to read, but it's there if you look hard enough. I'm everyone's favourite person when the zeros are accumulating in their bank accounts and bringing lots of lovely, easy money into their lives. Now, I'm avoiding everyone. I'm Matthew Kennedy, leper of the parish. Ding a fucking ling. Time to get out of Dodge, Matthew. I pick up a photograph of Angela taken on an island somewhere in the Caribbean a few years ago. I can't remember the name of the island, once you've been to one luxury island, they all seem the same after a while. Infinity pools, lobster dinners and shop talk over brandies. Same people, different location. Angela is looking out to sea in the photograph with her hair tied back and she is wearing no make-up. God, she's beautiful, she looks like she did when I first met her. I've fucked up royally there. I should have come clean about the vasectomy years ago. I didn't see that reaction coming. I thought she'd accept it and move on, maybe have a girly, we're worth it, weekend away somewhere tropical. We'd continue, the two of us, smiling out of the weekend supplements, making the rest of the world spill jam over our images on Sunday mornings, in jealous rage.

Got that one wrong, Matthew. I walk to the kitchen and

pour myself a glass of tap water. Christ, I feel rough. I knock back some Nurofen plus and sit down at the kitchen table waiting for the pain to go away. I look at my phone with its combination of missed messages and voice-mail messages. Forget it, Matthew, there's nothing you can do. I need to get my hands on some cash in the very immediate future. It's lucky I tucked some away before it all went pear-shaped. I can't even compute how little I've left and the thought of the miserable amount I have access to makes my head hurt again, so I press my forehead against the glass table. Angela hasn't returned any of my calls. My mother has been ringing continuously, dying to hear how far I've fallen. *Told you so,* that's what she can't wait to say. There's a knock on the kitchen door. I raise my head slightly, thinking I must contact Angela urgently as I need to discuss the house with her. Thank fuck it's in her name and no-one can touch it. I look around the kitchen and I'm working out that it will fetch four or five million easily, even with the property meltdown, when there's another tap on the back door, louder this time.

"For fuck's sake, do you have to knock so loud? Come in, whoever you are".

The door opens and the builder guy, Luke, walks in, dressed in a sports top, jeans and expensive trainers. He looks very fresh for six o'clock in the morning and there's such a strong smell of aftershave from him, that I almost throw up last night's dinner, well, if I had dinner. He stands over me at the kitchen table, a stupid smile on his face and says,

"The missus not here then?".

"She's gone shopping", I reply.

"At six a.m.? God, she must love shopping".

"Ha bloody ha", I say, "What can I do for you anyway?".

He fixes his hair and grins at me. He looks like a supermarket bargain version of James Dean. He says,

"I just need to get my final payment. I've finished with the garage conversion. A lovely gym for you and your wife now if I say so myself. If you want to recommend me to any of your mates, I have a card here".

He passes me a few of his business cards. I'd laugh if my head didn't hurt so much. He has a head shot of himself on it and such a posed look on his face, it looks like he's trying to be a male model. 'Luke O'Shea Construction – no job too small" is printed on it in a cartoonish font. I attempt to walk to my office to get cash from my safe. My head spins, so I lean against the kitchen counter because I feel like I'm on a roller-coaster.

"Rough night?", Luke-no- job- too- small, says, and I don't reply but he's a chatty fucker for so early in the morning and can't help the stream of words erupting from his mouth,

"I avoid alcohol these days. Wouldn't have such a great bod if I kept downing those kinds of calories. I had a quick jog on Dollymount this morning. Gets the blood flowing".

I ignore him and open the door of the kitchen that leads to my office when he says,

"Angela will love the sauna. You lucky fucker getting to share that with her every day".

I turn around and toy with him.

"Did you sleep with her?", I ask.

I can see the cocky fucker is debating whether to come clean or play it safe and get paid by me. The fact that he doesn't answer is proof enough for me, so I attempt to punch him but am so uncoordinated from the whiskey binge that I miss him by a mile. He grabs me in an arm lock and Mr. Nice Guy disappears as he says,

"Now, Matthew, if you guys in suits can't keep the wife ticking over, I kind of feel it's my duty to provide so to speak. I don't want any trouble here today. I just want to get paid for the work I did".

I try to speak but can't because my throat is constricted. He lets go and we walk to opposite ends of the kitchen, me breathing deeply, while he seems perfectly fine.

"Stay there for a second. I have a proposition for you".

He folds his arms and says,

"You and your wife love propositions, don't you? I'm not going anywhere. Not till I get paid anyway".

I remove some envelopes of cash from the safe and put two of them in my back packet. I check the one for Bob the fucking Builder and make sure it contains the right amount for the work we hired him for. Not a penny more. I hand him the envelope and he checks it.

"Right, grand. That's me done here. I'm off".

He walks towards the door, and I switch on the coffee percolator.

"You like your cash, huh, Luke? Nothing dodgy going on there?".

He hesitates at the door and says,

"Look, what I do with my money is none of your business. Just play nice and hand out my cards to your mates".

I laugh when I think that home gyms and saunas are not exactly going to be a priority for any of the people I know at this moment in time. I pull out a chair and say,

"Look, Luke, take a seat. Have a coffee? We got off to a bad start here this morning. And I get a bit crazy if I think my wife has been with someone else".

He looks suspiciously at me but sits down anyway.

"How long is she out this morning shopping, did you say?".

I reply,

"We don't need to worry about her. Let's just say that she won't be back for a while. Here's my proposition".

So, we sit and chat awhile and get almost pally, me and Luke who definitely slept with my wife and I pretend to listen to his protests about being clean for a while and that he doesn't want to go back inside again. I knew those muscles weren't developed on Dollymount Beach. But you know, I'm a people person and Luke is greedy like everyone else. When the extra envelope doesn't do the trick, I offer him one more and he accepts my proposal over a particularly nice cup of Italian espresso. I watch him get into his van and reverse down the driveway. I walk to the office, double check all the insurance paperwork and feel my headache start to clear as the sun streams through the window. Yup. House in Angela's name. Buildings cover in the event of fire damage. Perhaps it will be caused by an electrical fault. Standards certainly dropped in building these past years. Excellent. I have two days to clear the house before Luke earns his cash-filled envelopes. I can almost see the flames and smell the smoke.

CHAPTER 24

MARTHA:

I'm sitting in Gerard's office. He's gone out for the day, so I have the files all to myself. Dad says that Conor is locked in the past somewhere and someone needs to find the key to release him. I hope I can find the key. He spoke about his friend at the ill-fated party. The alcohol he usually seems to avoid allowed me to see through the layers he's built up around him over the years. The tattoo on his arm means he hasn't given up. I find the photograph of the group of orphanage kids and yes, that definitely is Conor at about eight or nine. The friend he has his arm around, blonde-haired and with a smile you know leads to fun, must be Francis who Conor referred to.

"Why did no-one ever adopt you?", I asked Conor on the way back to his cottage the day after the party. He was relaxed and happy, full of Dad's breakfast feast and flushed with a morning by the sea.

"I got too old, and no-one seemed to think I was worth the trouble", he said with no trace of self-pity.

"Did you ever trace your mother? You must be curious about her?", I asked.

I could see that he was beginning to shut down again, every mile closer to the Nursing Home brought him back to his default, solitary self.

"I always thought that if she gave me away, that was it. If someone throws something away, it usually means they're finished with it".

He closed his eyes then and fell into a sleep or a pretend one. I know when to stop asking questions. So, I'm in the office and I look through the files. I find a list of staff at the home at the time and take the file and the photograph of the children to the photocopier to make copies. I put the file back where I found it, put my copy in an envelope and place it in my handbag. I lock Gerard's office and put an end to my investigation as I walk to the wards to start my shift. The day crawls as I work out my next step and I feel a sense of relief when Dad asks me over dinner that evening why I'm so quiet. I take the photocopied documents from my handbag and pass them over to him at the table. He pats the envelope and says,

"Come on, Martha. Let's clear this table and we'll go to the balcony. It's a gorgeous evening. Let's see if the evening breeze can clear out the cobwebs and maybe we could work out a plan?".

We tidy up at a rapid pace and we carry coffee and shortbread to the balcony off the upstairs morning room, where a tiny cast iron table and two chairs await us. I've noticed a certain lightening in Dad's mood these last few weeks. When I sit beside him, I notice he's shaved today.

"Yep. I've decided to stop looking like someone on the F.B.I.'s most wanted list. God, it felt good to get rid of that scraggy beard, Martha".

I pour him coffee and say quietly,

"She would have wanted you to be happy, you know".

He touches my hand and says,

"Early days, Martha. Early days. Let's solve your mystery for you".

We sip coffee and come to the conclusion that Conor's friend had some kind of tragic death. Dad says he'll try and track down some of the people on the staff list.

"It'll give me something to do. There must be someone on that list that knows something. If they'll talk, that is. People are very tight-lipped when they decide to self-protect".

"What do you think happened?", I ask.

"We'll go through it methodically, Martha, and then see what happens. Are you sure you want to find out? Maybe Conor has his reasons for wanting to forget it all?", he says to me, pouring me a second cup of coffee.

"You know, I think I have to find out anyway. Take a risk. If Conor doesn't like what we find, we will just leave it there. But my instincts tell me I need to go ahead and find out", I reply.

Dad smiles, looks out to sea, and says,

"You are smitten, Martha. I know that look. I remember it well".

I begin to deny it and then decide to say nothing. Instead, I just sit with my father and enjoy the breeze on my face.

CHAPTER 25

ANGELA:

I am tempted to take notes while living with Lucy and Dave. They teach me so much about life and how normal life is so easy. Lucy is no angel. She bitches about housework, cranky kids and a husband who's glued to football on the telly, but she is content. Every day, while I'm here, from when Amy leans down to me on my camp bed beside her princess fairy bed and whispers loudly,

"C'mon Aunty Angela, let's get Coco Pops and paint our toenails", to when Dave eventually looks up from the T.V. screen to say to Lucy,

"You look tired, hon. Sit down here beside me, and I'll massage your neck",

I learn what it's like to be normal. Dave might still have one eye on his soccer hopes but he still notices that his wife needs her neck massaged from being in a cash office in a supermarket all evening. They don't do any of the big gestures which Matthew and I thrived on – the restaurant bookings, the exquisite bunches of flowers, the gift-wrapped boxes with tasteful pieces of jewellery. They don't need to. I try to avoid holding Jason, the baby, as I feel too raw still and it's the only time I feel any envy for Lucy. When someone passes him to me and plops him on my lap while they go on an errand and the baby wraps his arms around me, that's when I begin to unravel. So, after two weeks here, playing board games with Amy, watching movies with Lucy and basically taking up too much of their valuable space despite their protestations of *oh, no, Angela, stay as long as you want*, today is the day I leave. Lucy makes a half-hearted attempt every so often and asks me to ring Matthew, just to get closure. But she doesn't really mean it and we both know that ship has sailed and is an ocean away by now. I've been tracking the financial market on my laptop and from what I can gather, Matthew may need to find a new destination. The buzzards are circling, and he is deep in debt.

I pack my suitcase and fold the sheets and duvet carefully and place them on top of the camp-bed. Dave thinks I haven't slept well since arriving here, sleeping on the rickety camp bed with the mattress which dips in the middle. He thinks that I am a woman who is used to a high degree of comfort, and I can sense he is embarrassed by his humble home. I tell him that it is the opposite, that I have slept the best sleep of my life here in Amy's fairy-infested room. Company is a cure for the insomniac. I said goodbye to Dave and the children this morning. Dave has taken them around to his mother's to 'terrorise her' but I know he is being tactful and that he wants to leave Lucy and I to pack on our own. I can hear Lucy downstairs singing along to the radio and cursing occasionally when she disagrees with a caller on the talk show. I smile and complete my tasks. I climb under Amy's bed and place the large, gift-wrapped box containing the latest doll's house she has been requesting for months beside her little row of rainbow-coloured shoes. I smile as I imagine her screaming the house down in surprise when she finds it later.

I tip-toe to Lucy and Dave's room, place an envelope under each of their pillows – under Lucy's a weekend voucher for two people for three nights in Paris, all flights, accommodation, and expenses paid. I included a hand-written note to say that I will babysit the children for them. Under Dave's pillow, I have put in the envelope two tickets for him and Lucy to attend the Ireland v France soccer game in Paris next month. I am almost certain he will scream louder than Amy. I leave a wooden train set for Jason as he is a big fan of all things railway related. I gather my belongings and carry them downstairs. Lucy pops her head out of the kitchen and says that she will help me with the rest. After five minutes, I am set to go, my small collection of baggage a little sad, in the hall. Lucy says,

"I'm going to miss you, Angela, you know that?", and I
reply,

"But I'm only down the road and I'll pop in all the time. And
you are going to come to me, let me treat you and pour
wine down your gob?".

Lucy smiles but it is forced. I busy myself fixing my new,
shorter hairstyle. It's taking a while to get used to, but I like
the lightness of it.

"What's up, Lucy? You seem tense? Seriously, this rental
will be good for me. I need to be on my own for once in my
life. Maybe, shock everyone and get a job?".

I turn around to face her, smiling, but she says,

"Emm…Ange, remember when I said Anna was back from
Spain? Well, now, don't kill me, but I thought it would be
good for you to see her. You know as Oprah says, get
closure?".

I start to gather my possessions and say,

"Lucy. I love you. But no, I can't see her yet".

I've started to sweat slightly, and Lucy puts her hand on my arm.

"Angela, listen, I've been in touch with her. She's not well. There won't be much more time. You have to see her, you know...".

I interrupt her and say firmly this time,

"Lucy, I can't see her. I know you mean well but I can't face that woman. Not now. Maybe soon".

Something in Lucy's face changes and she looks at something behind me. I turn around and there she is, Anna, walking slowly from Lucy's sitting room and towards me. I step backwards to get away from her, but Lucy says, quietly, to me.

"She can't hurt you anymore, Angela. You need to get some answers from her".

I watch as Anna walks closer to me. She is old now; her hair is thin and she is skeletal in appearance and is unrecognisable. She leans towards me and says,

"Angela. I think we need to sit down and talk".

She puts her hand on mine and that's when I black out.

It's dusk in my cramped bedroom when it starts. I don't move the blanket because I am fearful of the bump that has grown larger these eight months. Arthur slapped me when he found out, said I'd be interfering with his income now that I was out of action. I reacted like a wild creature. I found energy I didn't know I had to scratch his face. He crumpled and retreated full of male bravado. 'I'll get you for this, you stupid bitch', as he ran off to the pub to meet his drinking cronies. Before he left, Anna spent ten minutes sorting out the scratches on his head. I could hear her tending to him, 'ah you poor thing, Arthur, Anna will sort you out, sweetheart. I know she is trouble. But we'll be rid of her soon'. 'OK, Anna, but she hurt me, look at my face'. I was laughing to myself when Anna came in and said, 'you've made a right mess of it now, you stupid girl, we'll have to figure out what to do with you now. Why are you laughing? There is something not quite right with you'. I slammed the door in her face and laughed some more at the thought of Anna thinking that I was the one with mental health issues.

Five months passed and I sat in my room mainly. I didn't even see Lucy. Tell her I'm busy, Anna. She'll tell her mother and that'll be it, you and Arthur will be found out. That did it. Anna shouting out through the letterbox, 'she doesn't want to see you, she's too busy'. Lucy wasn't buying it, but after a few months, she met Dave and I used to hear them laugh as they walked along the balcony, off on a date to the pictures or a disco and me hiding under my blankets forcing myself not to think about anything. I wanted my baby more than anything. I told Anna that so many times. She said, 'yeah, sure, course you can keep your baby', but I could tell she was lying and trying to figure out quick smart how to get rid of me. There was whispered talk of getting the fuck out of there, at night. I could hear them. The villa in Spain was bought and nearly ready to move into. 'Leave her here, Anna, someone will sort her out'. Anna was perky those few months, a pile of sundresses and swimwear building up on the chest of drawers in her room.

I ruined her plans by going into labour early. I was listening to my favourite Queen album on my record player and decided to kill some time dancing along. A fifteen-year-old girl, isolated in a single bedroom singing along with Freddie Mercury - 'Mama, just killed a man...' I used to fantasise that it was Arthur that Freddie was singing about.

240

But halfway through the dance, I felt a heavy pressure in my stomach and thought here we go. I sat there quietly for the next few hours thinking about what I could do. I packed up my suitcase mid-contractions and sorted through the little pile of items I had collected for my baby. Everything went a bit nuts after that. I stripped off and put on a nightdress and was thinking about trying to walk out with my suitcase and my best coat to try and find Lucy. Lucy will help me. Lucy will help me. I said this all the way through the next contraction. And then the pain got worse. And the blood came. And the screams from me that brought Anna to my room. She took over then. She took one look at me and said, 'You stupid bitch, this was not supposed to happen for at least a month'. She thought she'd be long gone. I know because I'd steam-opened her travel agent's letter with their plane tickets in it.

She put me back in the bed and said, 'Stop screaming Angela. They'll put you away somewhere. You are underage'. 'Bit fuckin' late, Anna', I said through gritted teeth. She calmed down a bit then and when I started to shout for Lucy again, she said to stop it, she can't help you, she's only a girl. I lay back on the pillows then, the pain too much and I couldn't think straight. Something's going wrong, I could feel it. Anna disappeared and I must have blacked out. When I came to, the woman everyone local called a midwife, was at my bedside. She placed her cold hands on my stomach. I moved away from her slightly, but she continued to press her hands to my stomach, saying, 'You girls, will you ever learn? Tut tut tut...'.

She held a drink to my lips, and I gagged when I smelt whiskey. I moved my mouth away from her, but she got Anna to hold me down and I was forced to drink it. It'll help with the pain. Drink it. Drink it. Like Alice in Wonderland falling down a hole. I don't remember much after that. I was being a 'good girl'. I remember they kept saying that. Only because I had stopped screaming by then. I thought of Lizzy. Oh, help me Mam, I said so many times that Anna and the midwife wouldn't look me in the eye anymore. 'It won't be long now', the midwife said and after what felt like days, the pain stopped and there it was.

My baby.

'He's not breathing', Anna said. The midwife just said, 'let me take a look and clear out his mouth, poor little mite' and then there were screams followed by silence and I held out my arms to hold my baby boy. But when I lifted my head, the room was quiet and empty. I heard a car pull up outside and Anna's voice issuing rapid instructions. The

midwife came back and gave me some tablets 'for the pain, sweetheart'. I spat them out and she put them back in my mouth. I swallowed them and went out cold. My final thought was that they'd stolen my baby.

CHAPTER 26

ANNA:

I lean against the arm of the sofa in Lucy's sitting room. I feel I shouldn't be here. I'm not welcome. I wouldn't have recognised Angela if I met her in the street. She's so different from the girl I knew. She's so glossy and self-assured. She's turned into a beauty. Lizzy would be proud. Tears come to my eyes when I think of what Lizzy missed, gone way too young with a packed-up liver. I'm going to have to take my chances when I see her soon, providing I end up in the same place as her. Lucy leans over Angela, holds her hand and whispers to her to wake up now please, it'll be OK. I step away from them as I feel like a spare part, and I need to take something for the pain. I walk to Lucy's kitchen, pour myself a glass of water and swallow the tablets down fast. That's all I do these days, take pills to stop the pain, but the pain is getting worse and there's talk of the Hospice for me now. I can't bear the thought of it, amongst all the good people with grandchildren visiting with home-made pictures decorating their headboards. I never got the chance to have kids. Arthur wanted none of it and well, I was thirty-five when I met him, and beggars can't be choosers. Some father he would have made, pimp for pre-teen girls all around our area. He was a bad egg. I can't blame him for everything, too much turning a blind eye to what was going on with Angela. I can only try and make it right now. I steady myself at the sink and can hear Angela talking now.

"I hope she's gone, Lucy", and Lucy calming her and saying *hush now sweetheart*, like Angela is a small child. I gather myself to face the music and just close my eyes for a moment, willing the painkillers to kick in.

There's no time to decide. Just a girl screaming, a baby boy howling and Arthur saying, 'get the baby the fuck out of here or I'll be facing time'. June, the midwife, was not getting involved. She'd got her payment and had done her job and was just having her cup of tea listening to Arthur panic. So, I hatched my plan. I waited till Angela was asleep and ordered a taxi. I dropped June home, 'you're doing the right thing, love, she can barely take care of herself'. I gave her an extra couple of notes just to keep her lips sealed. I asked the taxi driver to take me to St. Jude's, it was still going then, and I'd heard they didn't ask too many questions. The baby was as good as gold and I resisted holding him because I thought if I did, I might never let him go. I might pass him off as my own and me and Arthur could make a fresh start in Spain and be a proper family. Shows what my state of mind was like that night. Arthur was in the flat packing for Spain. The villa was due to be ready soon anyway and his mates would meet him for tapas in a bar somewhere and hand over our new identities to him.

So, I walked up to the door of Saint Jude's. It was a cold, winter's night and there was a scraggy Christmas tree in the hall and the sound of kids squabbling in the background. A nun arrived and took the baby from me. She accepted my story, poor girl got taken advantage of and the baby would be better off in a good home. There was very little paperwork. The taxi driver was impatient and charging me while he sat there, smoking, so I hurried out of there. Ten minutes it took. And twenty-four years for it to still stay in my mind and cause me lost sleep. I tried to help Angela get better before we left. She wouldn't even let me set foot in her room the next day. I put food in the cupboards and cash in the tea-caddy where she knew we left it. Took a taxi out to Dublin Airport with Arthur, 'you're going to love it, darlin' all that sun, get out of this kip of a country'. He was nervous as his small-time operation was getting out of hand and word was out about him. He'd be facing a jail sentence if he didn't get on a plane quickly and

*he only relaxed a few months into it when we moved into
our villa.*

*So, we lived our little life on the Spanish coast, me, Arthur,
and a group we hung out with, all running from something.
We had part-time jobs in hotels and bars and never heard
anything of home and Angela until the night the nurses
arrived. They were loud and full of Spanish wine, so they
didn't notice me hovering a bit too much around their table,
wiping down the already clean table. 'Poor kid', they were
saying, 'nasty business, but sure he had no hope anyway,
the home's closing soon, so they will be glad to retire those
nuns at Saint Jude's. Twelve years old and hung himself,
no-one knows why, well, they are not saying anything
anyway'. I wondered if it was him, the minute they spoke
about him. Made a call to June from a phone box and told
her to try and pass on the word to Lucy's mother. I got
drunk myself that night and still I didn't sleep, dreaming of
babies in taxis.*

"Anna, are you alright? Anna?".

Lucy is talking to me. I pull myself together and remind
myself of where I am. My breath goes slightly when I think
of Angela in the next room. I kept thinking that she'd have
married a good man and had a bunch of kids by now, but
life never works like that, all neat and set up to not

disappoint. Lucy puts her arm around me for support. It feels good to lean against her strong, young body and I tell myself to stop getting soft. She is not doing it for me. She just wants Angela to know the truth. Angela has gathered herself together and sits unnaturally straight-backed on the armchair. Her face is pale, and her hands are shaking.

"Anna. I don't know how you have the nerve to even look at me", she says.

"I'm so sorry…", I begin to say but she's having none of it.

She walks over to me, and her mouth is mean.

"You left me there, a fifteen-year-old girl, bleeding, confused and you took my baby. MY BABY. And left him in an orphanage. You never asked me, did you? You just wanted to get of there and keep Arthur happy".

Lucy says,

"Ange, maybe you could calm down, huh? …".

Angela continues as if Lucy was invisible.

"Do you have any idea what you did to me, Anna? You

248

passed me over to Arthur like I wasn't human, just something for men to use and discard when they were finished with me. The worst thing is that I trusted you. I thought you were Mam's friend. I thought you would keep me safe".

She puts her head in her hands and Lucy helps her back to the sofa.

"Drink this please, Ange, you are so upset", she says and hands her a drink.

I take a seat before I faint, and Angela laughs a strange laugh.

"Where's Arthur now, Anna? Found someone else, has he, now that you are not well and not able to run around after him, fetching him fags and booze and putting up with all his women?", she says.

"I'm done with men", I say quietly, and she laughs that strange laugh again and says,

"Finally, something we have in common, Anna. I've given them up too".

Lucy looks at her and says quietly,

"Anna has something to say to you, Ange. I know you can't stand the sight of her, but just listen to what she says and then you will never have to see her again. I promise".

Angela dries her eyes with the back of her hands, making her mascara pool in large blobs around her eyes. She's still beautiful, I think, not the fake beauty I could pull together in my hey-day, all make up and low tops and high heels to attract the wrong men. I breathe in and out and take a deep breath.

"I told June that he died when I heard those nurses talking about him. I know Lucy got the news to you and it could not have been an easy thing to hear".

"What? The baby I didn't want to give away hangs himself at twelve years of age. What do you think, Anna? It was the second worse day of my life and I..".

I interrupt her as I can't rest until I've said it.

"He didn't die, Angela. I got it all wrong. I found out later. The nurses were talking about the right home. But it was a different boy. Francis Doyle. Not your boy. Not your child. He's still alive".

Angela opens and closes her mouth, and nothing comes out.

CHAPTER 27

MATTHEW:

I think I might have got away with it. I'm staying in the granny flat, a glorified shed at the back of my parent's garden. How the mighty have fallen, etcetera. I've dumped all my phones as people have a habit of chasing you when you owe them money. I've bought myself a new laptop and am busy finding a way out of this mess. Angela's pretty boy did the job in the end. I rented a car for the day and parked it a few roads away. Luke banged the top of my car as he passed by, dressed in black, probably imagining he was in a Bruce Willis film and a little while later, I saw the satisfying sight of smoke. I've never spoken to him again. He's probably gone back underground, like the little rat he is. I turned up the music loud in my car and drove out of my life for the last time. Mum and Dad aren't too happy with me being back in their garden, probably desperately trying to work up some convincing story to tell their friends, bunch of back-stabbing, gossiping geriatrics. I'll be gone soon. There's enough to get me out of here and not to worry about money for a little while anyway. Once I get the insurance money, I'll be grand. Just the small job of trying to track down Angela so she can sign the paperwork and give me what's due to me.

I finally got a text back from her and she's meeting me at the beach in a few minutes. She's acting weird though. She said that she'd rather not communicate by mobile phone, that she'd prefer to see me in person. She's probably having second thoughts about leaving me, maybe it's not the end for us. I'll be back with new ideas soon and generating cash. It'll all be like before. That's what I keep saying to myself. If I say it often enough, I'll eventually believe it. I arrive at the beach and there's only one person on it. A woman with short, dark hair and wearing a casual jacket, jeans, and trainers. It's only when she gets close to me that I realise it's Angela. Well, a different Angela to the one I lived with. I am thinking that her hair suits her shorter when she says,

"Matthew. Hi". She smiles a pretend smile.

I realise then that I've been fooling myself all these years. Everyone thinks that I'm the one in control of Angela but she's the one in control and has always managed to keep herself apart from me. I'm suddenly nervous and not sure whether to kiss her or shake her hand. She leans over and touches me briefly on the arm, nothing intimate, like the way you'd touch a friend you hadn't seen in a while.

 I ask her,

"Can we go somewhere warmer, Ange? You know me. I don't like beaches unless they're in the Caribbean".

I try to act like I'm not bothered but inside my head I'm saying, I'm sorry, Ange, please don't leave me. Angela ignores me and keeps walking. I follow her, like a golden Labrador awaiting a treat from its mistress. Angela is talking and the Arctic wind makes it hard for me to hear her.

"I can forgive a lot of things, Matthew, but the vasectomy was the limit for me. I didn't deserve that".

She stops and faces me.

"I'm so sorry", I say and she talks over me.

"I'm so sick of that word. Sorry. Everyone uses it to me. I'm sorry Angela. I'm sorry Angela. For fuck's sake. People do what they want and then apologise. Too late, Matthew".

I stay silent for a beat and then ask her,

"I would have been a rubbish father, Angela. I know somewhere in your head you realise that. You would have left me then anyway".

"What happened with your company, Matthew? All those years, you and me putting up with all those people. Handing them drinks and putting up with all that shitty small talk. What the fuck happened?".

OK, it's this kind of conversation. I sigh and reply,

"It's over, Angela. That's all I can say. It's not my fault that the banks decided to over-react and fucked me over. I have got to get out of this country, Angela. I'm being hounded".

She looks at me and says,

"Did you burn the house down yourself? Or did you get someone else to do it? Some idiot who'll go to jail instead of you?".

"I didn't burn the house down. That's all you need to know. And no-one got hurt. You have to sign that paperwork. I need my half of the money. I really need it. I'm desperate".

She smiles and says,

"Now you know how I felt when we met in that hotel years ago. You'll do almost anything when you are desperate. Go home with a guy, marry him, sleep with his clients. Jesus, Matthew, get a grip. You haven't a clue, have you? The first time in your life you face a bit of shit and you panic".

She walks away from me, and I follow her, fuming.

"Well, you didn't exactly complain all those years, did you? You certainly enjoyed spending all the money and enjoying all the benefits. Not having a job to get up for every day".

"Being married to you was a job, Matthew. Trust me, I had to work very hard at it".

I know she's lying because somewhere along the line, our

256

marriage became the real deal for a while and we loved each other, even if we fucked it up in the end. Angela stops walking and says,

"You are going to ask me if I ever loved you. OK. Yes. I did. Not at first. And not at the end".

I touch her on her cheek, and she puts her hand on mine and says, softly,

"Oh Matthew. What have we done?".

"We could try, you know, see if it could work again?", and even as I'm saying this, I know it's all over.

Angela fixes her hair, looks away from me and says,

"It won't work now. Things have changed for me. Something new. Look, here's some cash for you. I had some put by. Take it to get away. I don't want to know anything about that fire and any part you had in it. I'll stick to what you said to write on the paperwork, that it was caused by an electrical fault and that's it. Here, take this too. You'll need it. I've set it all up for you. Travel documents, accommodation. It's all organised. I'll see you around. Fly safely. Icarus".

She hugs me and we hold each other for a few moments, listening to the sound of the sea in the background. She breaks free and walks briskly back down the beach away from me. I watch her disappear and when I can't see her anymore, I look at the folder she's given me. I open it and am startled by the destination on the travel documents. I wonder why my plane ticket is for a place in Africa I've never heard of. And then the proverbial penny drops. I race after Angela and when I arrive at the car park, it is empty except for my car. I get into the car, with a heavy heart, but smile for the first time in months. I'll go to Africa and give him a right shock. I'll come back when the dust settles and start all over again. Money always makes money. I'll find the magic again.

CHAPTER 28

MARTHA:

Dad has morphed into a private detective. He is just one deerstalker short of being Sherlock Holmes. He's been spending time on his computer getting closer to finding the addresses of staff who worked in the home around the time Conor was still in their care.

"It's the usual circle of fear and banished secrets. No one is willing to talk. I sense a cover up of some sort, Martha", he said.

If he had a pipe, I bet he would have lit it up then. I've been relegated to a Doctor Watson status and leave him with his files and his mystery to solve, content that he is becoming more engaged in the world again. He has started to play piano again, not just the desultory half-hour he had been doing for the last year, but hours of it.

"Helps me to think", he said, when I brought him coffee.

"Like Sherlock and his violin?", I remarked.

He didn't reply. He just smiled and played his music. I'm on early rounds today at work. There's the usual feel of anticipation around as it's Sunday and family visiting day. I catch up with Conor as he wheels Peter into his usual place by the window. It's Peter's regular Sunday vigil as he awaits his brother. Conor smiles at me when I place the two cups on the table and Peter says,

"Thanks, Martha. He's sure to come along today. I can feel it in my bones".

"I hope he does, Peter", I reply as I set out extra biscuits hoping Peter will at least enjoy some sugary treats this afternoon.

He doesn't look too well, all skin and bone and his skin is the colour of day-old snow.

"Where does your brother live, Peter? Is it far from here?", I ask him quietly.

Peter smiles and tells me,

"In my mother's place. He bought me out when Mam passed on. Typical Bernard! Good with money. It is worth a fortune now, but sure he never moved. It's in a lovely spot and Mam always said you could smell the sea on the clothes from the line, we were that close to it".

I tidy his shirt collar and smell the heated, faintly chemical smell from his clothes, as far from his mother's line-dried clothes as you could get. I stay with Peter as the cars arrive and he doesn't remove his gaze from the driveway as the sullen teens, dutiful children and assorted relatives make their way from their cars with gifts for their elderly relations.

"Old folk's gifts", Peter says, and he chuckles, "hard-boiled sweets and gardening magazines. Be careful, Martha, it happens to us all eventually".

I smile and he looks up at me and I see that he is a great actor, pretending to be hopeful but his eyes give it away.

Full of disappointment. I see Conor at the back of the room and become full of energy.

"Peter, I'll see you soon. My shift is over. I've a few things to do first but I'll come back and say goodbye to you".

Peter turns his head and sees Conor watching me, holds my hand and says,

"You two love birds. It makes me so happy to see it".

I blow him a kiss and walk up to Conor and ask him,

"Are you on early shift today?".

He looks at the clock as it turns towards 2pm and replies,

"Yes. You too? Have you something planned?".

I link arms with him, just as Tony arrives. Tony glares at me. He still hasn't got over the fact that I'm not interested in him but pity about him, as Peter would say. I'm not too worried about him as a beautiful, blonde Polish nurse has started this week and he is giving her the full charm offensive, muscles being offered for her evaluation every time she sits beside him in the canteen. She is a beautiful girl, but savvy with it and she seems quite taken by him. Maybe she'll take him on, and the rest of the female population can breathe easier. I walk with Conor towards Gerard's office. Gerard is outside in the hallway, performing his 'lord of the manor act'. He greets relatives and pats the heads of small children, in a slightly nauseating politician on the campaign trail manner. The clients seem to love it though. I wait until he is in deep conversation with the son of a couple who are residents here now (earning the son a double helping of Gerard's attention) and ask Gerard,

"Excuse me, Gerard, is it OK if I borrow the bus for an hour or two?".

He is in deep conversation about the vegetable garden and how much the mother of the man is enjoying it, so he doesn't pay that much attention to me.

"Hmmm…yeah, sure, Martha", he says, and I take that as a firm yes. I reckon I have about four hours until the bus is needed to bring the men to a bowling club a few miles away.

I smile at Conor and say,

"Conor, do you know how to drive a bus?".

He replies,

"What? Emm...I probably can if I tried. Why?".

I put my arm around him and instead of replying, steer him towards Gerard's office.

"Quick. Peter's file. I know we shouldn't, but I can't watch him sitting in that room of relatives anymore".

Conor smiles and we look at Peter's file. Next of kin is listed. Bernard. Excellent! I jot down the address, which is somewhere in Rush, about a half an hour's drive away and say,

"Fancy another trip to the sea, Conor?".

"Let's do it", he replies.

Fifteen minutes later, Peter is dressed warmly in his best coat, excited like a school kid on a day-trip. I left a note in the day diary – taken Peter for a Sunday drive- and hope that will buy us enough time to complete our mission. He was reluctant at first to leave his vigil at the window but when Conor leant close to him and said,

"Peter. We are going to bring you to see Bernard", his eyes lit up and we got him out of that room and into his own to 'spruce up' for his visit to his brother. We locate Rush quite easily, although the gear box may not survive Conor's assault on it. We get lost on some of the back roads and it's only when we arrive at the same crossroads we passed ten minutes earlier that we realise that we are lost. Peter looks out the window and admires the view of the sea. Conor and I look at the map but can't work out where we went wrong.

"It should be around here, somewhere, I'm sure of it", Conor says to me.

"It can't be that complicated to find Peter's house", I reply.

Peter perks up at the mention of his house and says,

"It's left here and then when you see a stone cross, you take a right".

Conor and I look at each other and laugh and I wonder at the ability we have to carry a compass for home, always.

"I thought the meds were making him a bit forgetful", Conor whispers to me.

"They normally do. But he seems OK. Let's follow his directions".

We drive until we see the cross on the road, and I look in the mirror to see Peter sitting up in his seat and when we take the right, he shouts,

"It's here. I'm home".

Conor pulls the bus in off the road and parks it at an awkward angle in front of a seaside cottage. It is a single storey cottage, slightly dilapidated, its white-wash façade faded but saved from complete neglect by a thriving rose garden. Peter is unbuckling his seatbelt and Conor walks around to the boot of the bus to fetch his wheelchair. While he is unloading it, I say to him,

"Maybe I'll go ahead first and just make sure that it's OK to visit before we bring Peter in. I don't want to disappoint him, just in case his brother isn't here or worse, you know, Conor?".

Conor replies as he wheels the wheelchair around to the passenger side of the bus,

"Don't lose heart, Martha. We did the right thing. It'll work out, you'll see".

I open the gate and try and ignore the excited voice of Peter as he is helped into the wheelchair. I walk up a weed strewn path and see that it leads to the back of the house. I hear voices from within, a female and a male one. *Please be Bernard*, I wish, as I tap gently on the door. A pretty, Filipino nurse greets me at the door and says,

"Yes. Can I help you?".

An elderly man stands behind her. His eyes are confused but I smile when I see that they are the exact same colour as Peter's and feel joyful that we have found Bernard. I show the nurse the ID badge which hangs around my neck. She nods.

"Hi. Yes. I'm Martha. I'm a nurse who looks after Peter, Bernard's brother in The View nursing home. We thought that Bernard would like a visit from his brother?".

The nurse smiles and says,

"Come in. I'll get Bernard organised for a visit and we can talk".

I walk behind her into a hallway, which has not been decorated for a few decades. Despite its disorder, it is a warm, welcoming home. Its walls are covered in photographs and every windowsill is groaning with seaside treasures. The nurse brings me into the kitchen and explains that Bernard has Alzheimer's and is house- bound these days. She reaches into a drawer and finds some letters, bound in string and I recognise the letterhead on the letters as being from The View.

"I wasn't sure what to do with these when they arrived. Bernard has a friend who deals with all his finances and bills, but somehow, we've never got around to all the paperwork, and these seemed to have got forgotten about".

She passes me one of the letters and I read the first one - Your brother, Peter, has been enquiring after you- and flick through the rest of them and they appear to say the same thing. My eye is caught by someone outside the kitchen window. Bernard, it appears, has managed to find his coat and is walking purposely towards the road. We place the letters back on the counter and follow him. Bernard stops on the path and in the distance, Peter can be seen, leaning on Conor for support, his wheelchair discarded by the side of the bus. Bernard's nurse walks up to him and stands quietly beside him as he suddenly calls to Peter,

"About time, Peter. Mam's been waiting on the beach a long time for us".

Peter walks towards him and hugs him tightly, saying,

"I knew you hadn't forgotten me, Bernard".

There is much laughter and a few tears from us nurses, and we get the brothers safely into the bus and I tell Bernard's nurse that we'll see her later. Conor beeps the horn in a goodbye gesture to her and the brothers whoop with delight. Conor squeezes my hand and says,

"I knew it would be fine in the end".

We drive them to the nearby beach and watch them as they sit on a bench, shoulder to shoulder in their winter wool coats, talking and laughing together. When it gets a little cold, we decide it is time to leave and drop Bernard back to his cottage, assuring him that we will visit again. The brothers hug, but they are tired after their reunion and Bernard walks slowly up the path, aided by his nurse. When he gets to the gate, he waves at Peter, his face full of happiness. Peter is smiling and Conor laughs as he repeats his old story,

"My mother used to take us out to the beach, the first chance of a bit of sun. We'd spend all day, me and my brother on the sand and we used to cry when it was time to leave. She used to say, well that was great, but it's time to go home now and she'd put cream on my burnt shoulders and say. Well, Peter, wasn't that the best day ever?".

He leans against the window and is asleep by the time we make it onto the main road. I check the time and realise that we better get a move on if we are not going to disappoint the bowlers back at the nursing home. As we pass the seafront, Peter wakes up and asks in a sleep-filled voice,

"Do you think it would be OK if we sit here for a while? It's so long since I've been to the seaside. Only if it's no trouble?".

As I'm a girl who was raised on the shore, I understand his reluctance to leave and say,

"Yes. Conor, do you mind pulling in here?".

He manages to park the bus eventually and his hairline is damp from the stress of driving a large, strange vehicle.

I kiss his hairline, offer him some water and he says,

"Thanks. I need a few minutes".

I wind the windows down so Peter can hear the breaking waves. He smiles and closes his eyes. The three of us sit for a long time, our eyes closed, enjoying the peace. After a while, I look at my watch, notice the time and say to Conor,

"We'd better go back. We'll be in a lot more trouble if we don't get the bus back soon. Are you all set, Peter?".

I turn around to check on him.

"Peter?".

Peter has passed away in one of those moments listening to the sea. I check his pulse and confirm my fears.

"He's gone", I say to Conor who has joined me at Peter's seat. He holds Peter's hand, cries silently and says,

"Oh Peter, I'm going to miss you".

I take Peter's other hand and we sit there, looking at his peaceful face and listen to the tide going out. My phone beeps and I read a text from Gerard,

-Martha? My bus? Call me, Gerard-.

I walk away from the bus as Conor puts a blanket around Peter and closes all the windows. I ring Gerard and when I connect to him, I have to hold the phone away from my ear as Gerard is not happy that he has a group of disgruntled men awaiting transport to their bowling club. He quietens down when he hears the reason and says he'll join us at the nearest hospital. I get back into the bus, fasten my seatbelt and find a route on the map to navigate us to a hospital. We arrive and some staff help us with Peter. We walk to an office and fill in some forms. As I am almost finished completing them, Gerard arrives.

"Martha?", he says, and I burst into tears and say,

"I'm sorry for borrowing the bus, Gerard. We just couldn't bear seeing him wait for Bernard anymore. It was breaking my heart".

Gerard pats my shoulder,

"It's OK, Martha. I won't go on about it. Too much. We'll just forget about the bus. What happened with Peter? Did his heart finally give up?".

I walk with Gerard to where Peter lies, on a bed in a curtained cubicle. I say to Gerard,

"Yes, he is the only patient I have ever had who died of a mended heart".

Gerard smiles sadly, says he'll sort out everything from here and suggests we get ourselves home. We say our goodbyes to Peter and walk back to the bus, holding hands. On the way back, Conor is quieter than normal. I put it down to shock and sadness, but when we are nearly home, he says that he needs to talk to me.

"OK. Will we go to your cottage when we get back? It's been a strange kind of day. A glass of wine would be lovely".

But while I'm talking about wine, Conor indicates, drives off the motorway and into a small country lane. He turns off the ignition and talks. I don't interrupt.

"I had a brother once. Well, he wasn't my real brother. We shared a room. We needed no-one else. We never fought like the other kids, only over comics and whose turn it was

273

to get the top bunk. Our favourite game to play was cowboys and Indians. We'd take it in turns 'Bang, bang, you're dead!', and we'd laugh so much at whoever's turn it was to be dead. The man turned up one day. One of the staff said we were being rewarded for good behaviour. I was nine, he was ten, Francis, my sort of brother. I don't remember much about the man. He was something to do with the money side of the home. He had a belt that jangled. I do remember that. Francis was excited. 'We're escaping for a day', he shouted. We sat in the back of the man's car. I can still smell it, fishermen's friends and Palmolive soap. He brought us to the countryside. 'Phew, the smell of cows', Francis said, holding his nose and the man looking in the mirror at him and Francis's hair lit golden in the sunlight. We played games on the hill. We brought our bows and arrows. We spent so much time just running. 'I'm aiming at your heart, Conor', Francis said, and he laughed so hard people stopped to look at the golden boy on the hill. The man just watched. After a while as it was getting dark, he said, 'Whoever wins the race, gets the Sheriff's badge'. I knew Francis was going to win. Even before we started running. The man said the prize goes to Francis my boy and Francis did a big whoop and ran towards the man. 'Where's my Sheriff's badge?', he asked. ' In my car', the man said, quietly. And I played on the hill - The Lone Ranger. They were gone for a long time, and I got bored and didn't enjoy being a cowboy when there was no one to shoot through the heart. They came back later to get me. Francis was quiet and looked at his feet. Clark's brown sandals, one buckle loose. 'Where's the badge?' I asked. But no-one answered".

CHAPTER 29

MATTHEW:

I awake in the granny flat, pushing off the flowery duvet for the last time. I make the bed well, tidy up, pack, and take a last glance at my work suits hanging up neatly in their plastic coverings. I shower using Mum's country garden vomit-inducing shower gel and shave with Dad's old-fashioned razor. He hasn't been influenced by ads with astronauts using scientifically-tested razor blades and am pleasantly surprised when his bog-standard razor blades do a great job. I wipe the foam from my jaw and hope that I haven't just noticed the start of jowls. Nah, I look again at my reflection and think, you've still got it! I'm bound to lose the weight from all those butter, cream and alcohol- fuelled business meals in the location I'm about to fly to. I laugh out loud thinking of what I'm facing. I smile at myself in the mirror at how like the town lunatic I must sound, laughing to myself in my parent's Parisian inspired bathroom. I grab my stuff, walk up the meandering stone path to their kitchen. Dad pops his head out and grabs one of my bags.

"Let me help you with that, son", he says and for fuck's sake, that's when I only start to blubber like a baby.

Dad fetches me a coffee and even though it's out of a jar, I drink it gratefully.

"You don't have to put on an act for me", he says.

"I know it's tough for you, Matthew. Just because half of Dublin are searching for you and their millions, it doesn't mean I personally hold it against you. You should have been more careful, Matthew. I don't understand this world, all this stuff that you all need. I'm from the generation that never borrowed. We just worked hard, saved our money and were happy with two weeks in Wexford, every summer. Everyone lost the run of themselves. All that spending and wanting stuff. Someone should have told them the difference between wanting and needing. Anyway, enough lecturing. I'm sorry about Angela. You treated her badly Matthew and I don't like that. We were brought up to look after the women….", he trails off, aware suddenly that he's said more words to me than he has in years.

I reply,

"Some women don't like to be looked after, Dad. Angela is one of them".

We do that awkward hug which Irish men do, a kind of leaning into each other, while at the same time being careful to not actually make bodily contact. I finish my instant coffee and get ready to leave.

"You know, I'll be back, Dad. I'm going to get it all back. The money, the business, the properties".

"And Angela? Will you get her back?", he asks, rising from his seat to join me.

I ignore the question and walk upstairs where I find my mother lying on her bed, fully dressed except for fluffy slippers on her feet. She has her eyes closed, but is not asleep and says,

"Matthew, I can't hold my head up high at the golf club, at the church, at the shopping centre, anymore. You've disgraced us. I hope you know that. All those people who trusted you with their money. All that...".

I interrupt her,

"They wanted more. It's as simple as that. I'm painted as

277

the bad guy here, but you know what? They were the ones who were greedy. Competing over houses and second houses, cars, and holidays. Don't blame me for other peoples' greed".

That gets her eyes open, and she says,

"Stop making excuses, Matthew. You made a mess. Of your business. Your marriage. Everything".

"Do you know, Mum? I don't remember you sending me back all those gifts I gave you when the money was flowing. Holidays, weekends away, meals in top restaurants. You're a hypocrite".

She slaps me on the face and then puts her hand to her heart. Always the drama queen. I leave the house and jump into a taxi. I've sold the cars. I need every penny and give the driver my office address. The building seems quieter now that half of the companies have disappeared. I press the button for the lift, but it doesn't seem to be working. There probably aren't enough people to pay the service charges anymore. I take the stairs and find myself out of breath halfway to my office. I open the door to my office suite, flick the lights on, walk to the window and have a look at the city I helped build. I see the cranes over West Wharf, and I wish it had all been different. Someone walks towards me, so I turn around and say,

"Hi, Laura. Thanks for coming in. I'm sorry".

She turns on me, saying,

"Sorry for what, Matthew? That you didn't pull it all off. Sorry for all the investors that you left me to fucking deal with by the way, some of them turned up here and were plain nasty. Sorry for leaving me with no salary for the past six months so I can't afford to pay my mortgage on the apartment I bought in one of your developments which you assured me was a smart investment. 400K for a shoebox. It's now worth about 300k and probably plummeting as we speak. No-one should fucking listen to you, Matthew. You are a snake-charmer, a cheap dollar and dime salesman. It's all bullshit".

I watch her as her face grows redder, wait for her to calm down and say,

"Laura, just sit down and let me talk to you for a few minutes. I'm leaving the country in three hours".

I can see that she is hesitant but guide her over to where the seating area is. I hand her a folder.

"In there, are cheques made out to Walsh, Hennessy, and O'Brien. It's a fraction of what I owe them. Can you get it to them, please? That's all I can do. It's up to them if they want to pay any of the builders who are out of pocket from when the building stalled. There's a cheque for the rent on this place for the next few weeks and that is it. I can't afford to renew the lease on the office. It's over, Laura. The last cheque is for you. It's a small figure, I know, but it might help you pay some of your living expenses for a short while".

She looks at the cheque and laughs,

"A month, max. Christ, I don't know what I'm going to do, Matthew".

"You'll do what everyone else is doing. Just get up and face each day and plan the next move, Laura. Right, I'm off. Thanks for all your work over the years and good luck with everything".

I take one last look at West Wharf, close the door of my office and don't react when I hear Laura's last words. I've heard them too often lately. I hail another taxi and go to Dublin Airport. Icarus is in transit.

CHAPTER 30

ANNA:

I've spent a life amongst noise. I only realised that after I'd been here a day or two. Flats and villas are busy places, full of everyone's problems and noise, loads of it. I haven't decided yet if I like the silence. At first it made me a little nervous, like when I was little and my brother, Jim, used to jump out and give me a scare, for the fun of it. I think of Jim a lot these days. I find I've gone way back in my mind and think of Mammy, Daddy, me, and Jim, all cooped up in a flat that smelt of Dettol and some sort of stew Mammy was always cooking. She was a Leitrim woman and never quite adjusted to the city. You can see it in the photographs. She was healthy and wholesome in her wedding photo, a happy young girl looking up at my dad, his hair slick with Brylcreem. His eyes were full of love and wonder for the country girl who honoured him (that's what he always said) by becoming his wife. The city withered her. In all the photographs after the wedding ones, she gets thinner, and her mouth is set with a slight dissatisfaction. She loved us, that's for sure and she loved my gorgeous docker dad. I wonder about my little brother Jim and how he is in London now. Last time I saw him, I barely recognised him, and his accent had become dimmed and replaced by a London twang. He and his doll like wife, Tracy, with her peroxide blonde hair and their children, twin boys with Jim's grin from childhood and Tracy's lovely manners.

A lady comes to check on me. She has gentle hands and massages cream into mine which are knotted and rough from years of putting my hands in sinks. She has a gentle voice, like a radio presenter and she makes me feel calm and relaxed as I prepare for 'the last moments' as they refer to it here. I'm not used to such gentle ways. My life was always dirty and loud. No-one spoke in gentle tones.

You've done the right thing.

The thought pops into my head every so often. I berate myself for allowing myself such a good thought. I only did the right thing after doing the wrong thing for so many years. I went to Lizzy's grave before I checked in here. I fool myself that it's a sort of retreat and I'm only here until I feel a little better. There is no check-out date available here. I placed pink roses on Lizzy's grave, the type a boy would give to a girl at Clery's clock, on a first date. We never had those kinds of dates, me and Lizzy, but it never stopped us hoping that someday we might meet a boy who would treat us well and open doors for us. It was hope that killed a lot of women where we came from. Lizzy didn't get to see how beautiful Angela has become. Her kidneys were 'screwed' as she said to me at the hospital when I last saw her. I asked her for forgiveness at the grave and left the flowers there. The sun shone through the clouds as I started to walk away. I took that as a sign that she was smiling at me. Foolish woman, clutching at straws and hoping sunbeams are full of dead friend's forgiveness. I hope Angela has found him now. Her boy.

I handed him over to a nun at reception that horrible night and she said she'd process him. She had cabbage in her teeth, I remember that. A tall nun too, which was unusual. The nurse in Spain said that the home was run by different people. I should not have passed on wrong information and let Lucy find out third-hard that Angela's boy had died in a tragic accident. I had stood on the balcony of the villa, smoking a cigarette, and thinking, this could be it, Anna, it could be all over, for everyone. So that's what I did, in a few phone conversations, even though I should have checked the facts first. When June, the old midwife said,

"Is that what they called him then, Anna? Francis Doyle?".

I hesitated for a minute, knowing I wasn't one hundred per cent sure. But I took the easy way out and replied,

"Yes, June, he was called Francis".

When I found out later that I had got it wrong, I consoled myself by thinking that they would have found a lovely home for Angela's baby. I just didn't want that old trouble turning up again in my life again, not when I was so happy in Spain. I made Angela think that she had lost her boy, again. Twice, Anna. You took her boy from her twice. I press the buzzer by my bed again. A nurse arrives and talks to me so quietly that I can barely hear her. My hearing is going, and they said it would be the last thing to go.

"Let's get you sorted out and tidied up, Anna".

I relax and lose myself in a morphine sleep. I can smell bread baking, like the one Mammy used to make. Maybe, I can finally make it home.

CHAPTER 31

ANGELA:

He is still alive. He is still alive. I lie awake in my new house. Everything is brand new, freshly purchased with little thought put into it. I arrived here the day after Anna gave me the news. Lucy and Dave helped me move in. I have few possessions. I spent two hours in a store purchasing it all and it arrived in one delivery - beds, sofas, furniture, pots and pans. I've never lived on my own before and find it strangely peaceful. I live in a box type house; square rooms which are clean and the house has one and a half bathrooms. Everything is basic and functional. Fresh page, clean slate, new chapter. I sit at my kitchen table which overlooks the tiny, patio garden. A robin sits on the wall, his eyes ever searching. He watches me as I sip coffee and I take this as a good omen. I'm not sure why, but I am open to superstition and old wives' tales in my current state. If I see a rainbow, I take this as a sign that he will see me. If a black cat crosses the road in front of me, this can send me into a dark mood which propels me back

to bed and I can waste hours with the negative thought –
he will not want to see me. I am afraid that he will ask me
why I didn't go to find him when I got married to Matthew.
Then I'll have to explain my early years with Matthew and
why I was afraid to look for him and just hoped he was with
a good family. Today, I am in a nervous state of mind. My
stomach churns and I have butterflies, like a girl awaiting
her birthday party. I fan the birthday cards on the table.
One to twelve. Birthday boys on tractors and skateboards.

I never purchased a thirteen-year-old one. That's when
Lucy told me. Matthew and I were at the races, and he had
just won big on a horse. There were long odds, and no-one
thought it would win. It beat the field by a good distance.
Typical Matthew, everyone said. He was the golden boy
then and the win transformed the party into a champagne-
fueled frenzy. Lucy phoned and said, "Can you talk?". and
I rang her back from the back of the stand. Life has a habit
of locating you no matter how good your day is going and
ignores the fact that you are married to a golden boy.

"Anna has found out that your boy has passed on, Ange.
He was called Francis".

I didn't speak and the rest of the conversation became a
blur of condolences and the words 'tragic incident'. Lucy
knew that I had been debating whether to tell Matthew the
truth about the baby and poured cold water on my fantasy
of bringing him to live with us, knowing full well that
Matthew would never agree. I held the phone to my ear,
but I was frozen, and Lucy kept saying, 'so sorry, Ange,

are you OK?', when Matthew arrived and said,

"How can you look sad on such a fantastic day, Ange?".

I disconnected Lucy's call and he spun me around to everyone's delight, the beautiful couple dressed in Brown Thomas limited edition fashion, embracing at the races. I kept my smile all day, drank two people's share of champagne, stripped down to my Italian lace lingerie and continued the illusion of the perfect wife. Matthew was asleep within seconds, but I crept to the spare room and looked at the birthday cards which I had never sent. I got up the next day, made coffee for Matthew and buried the thought of my son in the dark place where I kept Lizzy and Anna. Today, my boy is resurrected. He's back from the dead, free to escape from the place in my mind where I've buried him. I can't sit still, and I have some time until Lucy arrives. I walk into the second bedroom and spend time imagining him in this room, trying to erase the image of a twelve-year-old boy and replacing it with the reality of a twenty-four-year-old man. My son. I never even got to name him. I sit on his bed and have imaginary conversations with him.

I was only fifteen. I don't know who your father was. I never looked at their faces. The conversations end in my head with the words - sorry, sorry, sorry. He won't be grateful for my sorrow, the boy whose mother gave him away. My doorbell rings and I open the door to find Lucy standing on my front step, dressed in her best outfit which she bought for Jason's christening – a rustle of blue silk fabric. She hugs me quickly and I say,

"Coffee, Luce?", but she's already walking back to her car. I grab my coat and handbag, lock the front door, and join her in the car. Lucy turns to me, tears in her eyes and says,

"I can't wait any longer, Ange. I am a nervous wreck. I didn't sleep at all last night, thinking of him somewhere out there waiting for you to find him. I'll be fine in a minute. I just need to take some deep breaths".

"It'll be fine", I reply, taking her hand in mine and we both laugh nervously at the situation we are in.

Lucy fumbles in her over-sized handbag, removes packets of children's' sweets and miniature toys in a fit of impatience, places them on her lap and says,

"It's in here somewhere. Underneath all this junk. Hold on, I've found it".

She hands me a card with 'Angela' written on it in her best handwriting. I open it and smile when I see the 'It's a boy' baby congratulations card.

"I know it's stupid, but I never got to buy one for you before and I was just so excited for you and then….".

She doesn't finish her sentence as she starts to cry. I take some tissues from my bag and dab at her eyes.

"Thanks, Angela", she whispers, "you are very calm. No tears at all?".

I take her make-up bag from her and re-apply her eyeshadow and mascara.

"If I start, I'll never stop, Lucy".

We look at each other for a second and she attempts to compose herself in the mirror and says,

"Thanks, Ange. I look nearly human. Nearly good enough to marry Andrew Ridgley, huh?".

I smile and put Lucy's card into my bag, and we drive off, two hours early for our appointment. We park in the carpark of The View nursing home and watch the nurses bring people into the garden. Two elderly ladies in vibrant colours talk animatedly as they are pushed in wheelchairs to the garden. They argue and laugh and eventually settle to their task of pruning roses.

"That'll be us in thirty-years", Lucy says.

I look at the lady in purple who wears bright pink lipstick and say,

"You'll be the lady in purple".

Lucy laughs. We sit for another hour, watching the procession of people, willing the clock to move forward to eleven o'clock. At quarter to, Lucy can't stand it anymore, removes her seatbelt and says,

"Come on, let's go".

Now that I am here, I feel frozen and stay in my seat for five more minutes. Lucy marches around the car park, a ball of nervous energy, her blue silk dress billowing around her legs. I get out of the car and walk towards her.

"You can do this, Ange. It'll all be good, in the end".

She looks doubtful and I try and ignore her fear. We walk into reception, talk to the young girl sitting there and she tells us to take a seat. A few minutes later, her phone rings. She talks for a minute and then tells us to follow her. We walk down corridors which are painted in magnolia. Although it appears calm and modern, I wonder if it is just my imagination or does it still feel like an orphanage. I become panicked when I wonder if it was a happy place for him but squash the thought as a middle-aged man with kind eyes greets us at the door of an office with a manager sign on it.

"Call me Gerard", he says.

We introduce ourselves and he says,

"Take a seat, ladies".

We sit down on the chairs, and he says,

"I'm so pleased to meet you, Angela. I may be able to solve the mystery for you. First of all, I just need to call one person into the meeting if you don't mind?".

I nod my head as speech seems to be beyond me.

He presses a button on his phone and says,

"Great! Yes, send her in, please".

The door opens and a beautiful young nurse walks into the room. She has wavy, blonde hair which is tied in a ponytail. Her eyes contain the hint of tears and when she sees me, they light up.

She walks towards me. I remove my hands from my lap and attempt to shake her hand, but she ignores it.

To my surprise and Lucy's, she puts her arms around me, holds me tight and says,

"I am so pleased to meet you, Angela", and then she bursts into tears.

CHAPTER 32

MARTHA:

Dad and I walk the beach early this morning. It's cold out here at dawn and we link arms to provide some body heat. Today is the day. In an hour, I will get into my car and drive to Conor's cottage. I told him that he may be better off on his own today, but he asked me to help him prepare the cottage. Dad has hung up his metaphorical Sherlock Holmes deerstalker. He printed off some information for me, placed it in a file and it is in my handbag, an unexploded bomb awaiting ignition. Gerard thinks it's up to the mother and the police to decide what to do with the information. Mr. X, as my father and I refer to him, better be enjoying his last days of freedom. When I arrived back home after taking Peter on his last trip, exhausted and tearful, Dad said that he would find out all the information I needed. I have the name of the accountant or in Conor's words,

"I don't remember much about the man. He had something to do with the money side of the home".

Conor didn't elaborate much on what he told me in the bus. But the wheels are in motion and his tattoo will eventually become fact. I gave Angela the files and told her as much as I could. She was quiet but I sense she is a tough person. I talk to Dad about the boy, Francis. Dad tells me that the unwatched over children often become the target of abusers. Gerard has traced as much information as he can, but old loyalties are in place amongst former workers of St Jude's and silence on telephones has become commonplace. Secrets and lies are buried deep. The family of Francis must exist somewhere and with the right research, Dad hopes they will come to light, eventually. I don't know the circumstances of how Angela has come to find her son, but I am so happy that they are to be re-united. Dad says to remain cautious as I have a tendency to require Hollywood movie endings, but I ignore him because this story is going to end well.

I get ready to go to Conor's, thinking I am doing well and remaining calm, until I arrive at the kitchen and Dad reminds me that I do not have a shift, that I don't need to wear my uniform. I look down at my nurse's uniform and slap my head in an idiot gesture. Dad laughs and has coffee ready for me when I come back down in a festive outfit. I am wearing a floral mini-dress and my purple converse trainers. It is definitely a day for wearing your best outfit. I drink my coffee, kiss Dad on the cheek and pack the new file into my bag. I hear Dad playing the piano as I leave the house and know it's a regular activity recently and that it will not be long before he can't resist the lure of touring again. Mum would be proud. Conor is nervous when I arrive at his place. He paces the sitting room floor and because I become slightly dizzy watching him, I suggest we take a walk in the woods behind his house. He looks around his cottage and is hesitant to leave. The house is gleaming. Every surface is polished and despite his concern that he doesn't have the correct food for his mother (he says 'mother' in such a low tone it is barely audible), I tell him that the food on his kitchen table is enough to feed an army. He has purchased two different types of teas and coffees, three varieties of biscuits and along with the scones I brought from home, I tell him I think we have it covered. From what I have seen of the beautiful and extremely slim Angela, I doubt she will eat anything. She has that kind of hourglass figure that I dream of, which involves sacrifice and a mathematical brain to calculate calories. She is very young. My first instinct was that she looked too young to be Conor's mother but worked out that she must have been about fifteen when she had him. She is definitely Conor's mother; her beauty confirms that, dark haired and green-eyed and they both have the same wary look. Perhaps their lifetime estrangement has led to that particular look, and it will wear off in time. Or maybe I am looking for the Hollywood ending with violins playing. It can be very difficult to be an optimist in this cynical world, but I will continue to expect the best from everyone.

I have to almost run to keep up with Conor as we walk in the woods. He is wearing his good clothes today as well. I catch up on him as we get to the old graveyard and find him standing at the same white cross in the infants' part of the graveyard. I sit down beside him, which proves a little difficult in a mini-dress and look at the grave he always seems to be drawn to. I read it and realise that I have read it before, the day I walked to his house with him. 'Francis Doyle b. Jan 3rd, 1984'.

I say to Conor,

"They buried him with the babies?".

He takes some time to reply.

"He had been really quiet for a while. I couldn't talk to him, because every time I tried to, he ignored me and said he was too busy. He took his own life, hung himself in the bedroom we shared when I was out playing soccer with the other boys. I can never forgive myself for that, me laughing and joking when Francis was sitting on his own in the room with all those horrible thoughts".

I say quietly,

"You were only a small child yourself, Conor. You couldn't have understood what was going on. Some adult should have stepped in and noticed what was going on".

"I offered to go in his place", Conor says, "he told me to piss off and mind my own business and that it was no wonder no-one ever wanted to adopt me, I was an annoying little git. I dream about him all the time, Martha. I can't get his face out of my mind. I don't think I ever will. I let him down and he died on his own".

I touch him gently on the arm and say,

"Maybe you are looking at it the wrong way. Have you ever thought about it in a different way? Maybe you were the only good thing in his short life. His brother like you said?".

Conor is quiet and says,

"Maybe you're right. We'd better get back to the cottage. It must be nearly time".

We walk back to the cottage, hand in hand and just as we get there, I say to him,

"Gerard will say that we should give him a proper burial, that we can't leave him there in the infants' grave. He should have a proper headstone this time with the date he died written on it, not hidden, and forgotten about so no-one will ask questions?".

Conor replies,

"Yes, we have got to do that. Maybe beside Peter? He'd have loved Peter. They were alike, full of fun and mischief. They'd be kindred spirits".

Conor kisses me and says,

"Thanks, Martha. For everything".

I kiss him back and we say nothing more. A car weaves its way down the driveway and stops outside Conor's cottage. Before he gets a chance to say anything, I say goodbye and good luck in a whisper to him and walk briskly back to my car, leaving him to meet with his mother.

CHAPTER 33

ANGELA:

I drive along oblivious to all the other drivers on the road. I pay attention enough to avoid collisions, but my head is spinning. I pulled in a while ago to ring Lucy. I told her that I thought I was having a heart attack. She laughed and said I wasn't going to have a heart attack at the age of thirty-nine, that I was just nervous. I am terrified. That he'll hate me, that he won't talk to me, that I won't know what to say to him, that he'll ask me why I gave him away, that he'll ask me who his father is. Shut up, Angela. This is a good day. I calm my breathing and think about the fact that I have a twenty-four old son awaiting me. I have never had a relationship with a male before that wasn't a tainted one. I don't know who my own father is and I never had brothers or uncles or a grandfather. I am afraid that I won't know what to say to him. I try to focus on what Lucy said. Be yourself, Angela. The problem is I am not exactly sure who that is. I have never really been myself. I was Mam's carer and pal, Anna's housekeeper and chief earner, Matthew's wife. I will need to find a new me. Or maybe the real me. Lucy said I'll know what to say when I meet him, that motherhood is instinctive, but I worry that doesn't apply twenty-four years later. I really liked the girl, Martha. She is so pretty and so warm and natural and she has a thing for my son. There it is, my son, in a sentence. I smile so widely that an elderly man in the car beside me smiles back at me. I take the turn for the nursing home and my heart starts palpitating again, but I force myself to keep calm. I park outside the cottage. It looks pretty and well looked after. The gutters look like they need a good clean, mind. I laugh out loud, thinking I've started to think like a mother already when he walks outside.

He is about five foot eleven and he has short dark hair, cut close to his head. He is dressed in black, and he squints into the sun, his hand over his eyes shielding them from the light. I get out of the car, smooth down my trousers, briefly noticing that my hands are slick with sweat and walk towards my boy. He steps towards me into the shade and takes his hand away from his eyes. They are green, just like mine and Lizzy's. He is nervous as I can tell from the way he holds his mouth closed tight. This changes when I say,

"Conor?", and he smiles, and his eyes become full of joy, and I walk towards him, hesitant at first. But like Lucy said, motherhood is an instinct and something about this beautiful boy is fragile and lonely, and I put my arms around him, inhaling his scent for the first time in twenty-four years and say,

"I have missed you every single day".

We stand there for a long time, arms wrapped around each other. Conor pulls away first and I remind myself to take it slowly. I watch him as he walks into the house and he puts his hand through his hair in a gesture that is so familiar to me as Lizzy did it all the time and say to him,

"Your grandmother would have loved to have met you".

He smiles and says,

"Would you like coffee? Or tea? Or both?", and I follow him through to his kitchen which is immaculate and laden with food and reply,

"Whichever you prefer? Do you drink tea or coffee?".

He picks up a teapot and I sit down and marvel over this first fact about my son. My son, Conor, is a tea drinker. I don't know what age he was when he got his first tooth, or what age he was when he walked, or talked or fell in love with a girl, but I know he is a tea-drinker. That will have to be enough for now. We sit and drink our tea and I tell him some of my story. I try to be honest, but I don't tell him too much, in case he is shocked and doesn't like me or want to see me again. He is guarded too, and I can gather after a half-hour of his company that we are quite similar, for two strangers, who just happen to be mother and son. I try to change the conversation after a while, especially when he doesn't elaborate much about Francis. I attempt to keep my voice light and airy when I ask him if he was ever harmed by anyone.

"No", he replies, and I try to hide the relief in my voice and ask him to show me around his lovely cottage. I walk to his sitting room and find his wall of photos. It is in here that I lose my calm demeanour, when I see that he has placed my teenage photo at the centre of the wall. I touch the photo and say,

"I'm so glad they gave it to you. I was fourteen when my friend Lucy took that photograph. It was before my Mam was taken away".

I look at my happy face and the hope that was in it and I say to Conor,

"You will love Lucy. She is dying to meet you. She and her family took me in after you were born and took care of me

302

for a while".

He looks at me like he has a thousand questions to ask, and I know that if he lets me into his life that we could have a lifetime to talk. We don't need to find out everything today.

I ask him,

"Did you get other stuff from me? I put things into a box for you. I know it was gone because when I collected my stuff from Anna's flat, I couldn't find it".

He replies,

"Yes, I have it in the kitchen".

He walks to the kitchen to get it and brings me the old Odlums box where I had stored my precious gifts for him. He removes the tiny cardigan I knitted for him and never got to dress him in. I see the dog-eared copy of' The Selfish Giant' book, which I had bought, in my innocence, to read to him. I hold the baby cardigan in my hand and smile.

"I was never much of a knitter, but I just wanted you to have something from me".

He says,

"I always kept them near me. You know, I always thought that I'd never get to meet you and that these few things would be all I had from you".

We both stand there for a while, heads down admiring the cardigan that I struggled to knit night after night and I look at the box and say,

"Those other items. Are they important to you too?".

He hesitates for a moment and says,

"I'm not sure if you have much time. I kept some things from when Francis died and I don't know, maybe I thought someday, I could find some answers".

"I have time", I say,

We sit and he tells me the story about being taken to the hill in the countryside by the man. I touch his hand gently when he finishes speaking. I am struggling to find words to say to him when I notice a piece of paper lying on top of the box, pick it up and ask him,

"What's this, Conor?".

"It's part of the registration number from the man's car", he replies.

I say as calmly as I possibly can,

"Can I keep it for a while?".

He looks me in the eye, leans back in his chair and says,

"Yes".

CHAPTER 34

MATTHEW:

I awake in a sweat. Well, I awake in a sweat every day, so nothing new to report there. I've landed in hell. Or heaven if you listen to my do-gooder brother. I'm sticking to Angela's terms. She won't tell anyone about the house insurance scam if I stay here for at least a year. She doesn't realise that it suits me to hang around here as I need to make some plans. She sent most of the money from the insurance company, anonymously, to my brother's charity in West Africa. I did my best to try and get it back, but it was too late. It was all processed in Angela's name so there was no way I could get involved without raising suspicion. James is over the moon. He doesn't know the origin of the money. He is delighted as he gets to fulfil his dream of self-sufficient villages all over Africa with all that money. He met me at the airport in his khaki shorts and bright yellow charity t-shirt and said,

"About time, bro. Sometimes we need to leave the rat-race".

I didn't think it was the right time to tell him that the rat-race had left me, so for the past few months, I have gone along with his charity lifestyle. He has a Scottish wife, another doctor, called Tara and they live in a tent right next to mine. I have lost half a stone already and I am starting to finally feel like I won't die of heat exhaustion by sunset each day here. In a bitter twist as everyone knows that I'm allergic to children, James has put me in charge of teaching in the village school. I loathed it at first, but weirdly, the kids here seem to love me and follow me everywhere.

"'You're a natural", James said after my first morning teaching.

He obviously didn't pay attention to what I was teaching them, because I gave the five-year olds a crash course in basic economics. Frankly, I think it went right over their heads. I move around in my tent, and I hear James and Tara outside speaking with their chirpy voices about it being another beautiful day. Their happiness is relentless.

"Come on, Matthew, your turn to go to the well", James says.

I unzip my tent and say,

"I would sell my soul for a coffee machine".

James laughs and replies,

"If you had a soul".

He claps me on the back and walks to the well with me. There is never one morning when he doesn't lecture me about how important water is here. I haven't got the energy in this heat to tell him that he has told me this about seven hundred times and do what I have done since I got here, just get on with each day. I hear the sound of kids laughing and turn around to watch them walk towards the village school, full of energy and rearing to go for another day. I sigh. Seven months, Matthew. I can stick it out. I can go back to Ireland then and start again. Find some money, start the whole ball rolling again. There'll be a killing to be made once the house prices hit rock-bottom and I will be even richer next time around. And I will win Angela back. She'll come around. She loves me really. And sure, don't we all have secrets and past lives that we want to forget about? Even Angela and the fact that she never explained the fax from the fertility clinic where she had ticked the box - Have you had a previous pregnancy? – and answered with a 'yes'. I'm lost in thought at the well. Standing beside my brother and he smiles at me and says,

"Here they come, Matthew. Your fan club".

The children line up outside the school and I walk back down the hill carrying water and think about what I am going to teach them today. I walk towards them. They cheer. Seven more months. It'll go by fast.

CHAPTER 35

MARTHA:

Today, we say goodbye properly to Francis. Gerard got permission to move him to the new graveyard and he is being buried beside Peter. It's been six months since Conor and Angela were re-united and I have had to learn to be patient. Conor spends nearly all his time with his mother, and she is trying to get him to move with her into her new house. Conor cannot quite accept that she wants him. He has spent his whole life convinced that his mother discarded him. It's going to take time. Angela is paying for him to re-sit his exam so that he can do what he is best at, dealing with the patients here at The View. I am so happy about that, because when the first flush of excitement was over when they had met again, I was afraid that she may take him away and move somewhere else. My father has come with me for Francis's funeral. He is curious about Angela and flushes slightly when he meets her. I've noticed that all men have this reaction to her, but from what I can gather, from Lucy, Angela's friend, Angela has had enough of men for the time being. She wants to concentrate on being a mother. She walks up to me at the graveyard and says,

"Martha. You look lovely. I just want to say that I am so glad that Conor met you. He is very taken with you".

Conor overhears her and smiles. He is still becoming accustomed to the embarrassment of mothers. Angela whispers into my ear,

"I am so grateful to you, Martha. I can never thank you and your father enough".

I reply,

"You're welcome".

She holds my hand, squeezes it and smiles. Gerard and the priest arrive, and we take our place at the graveside. There has been a headstone commissioned with Francis's photograph to feature on it and the record of his date of birth and death. Gerard told me that there is to be an official enquiry. When I told my father this, he said,

"Good".

He is secretly pleased with his detective skills. Conor reads at the graveside from the book his mother gave him twenty-four years ago. All is quiet here as he reads from the book and speaks,

"And the other children, when they saw that the Giant was not wicked any longer, came running back, and with them came the Spring…"

CHAPTER 36

ANGELA:

I dress carefully today. I put on a dress which flatters my figure. I have grown used to wearing comfortable clothes in my new life and find the tightness of the dress restricting. I put on a pair of stilettos which Lucy leant me. I spend time applying make-up and recognise the old Angela when she appears in the mirror in front of me. I brush my hair, still short, and apply hairspray to it. While I'm applying lipstick, Conor peeks his head around the door and says,

"Bye, Angela, we're off".

I blow him a kiss and say,

"Have a great time, you two".

Martha says,

"Thanks, Angela, you look very glam. Off somewhere nice yourself?".

I lie and say,

"Yes, off to town, you know yourself, we all need a bit of glamour every so often".

Conor holds her hand, and they leave, shouting as he goes,

"Don't wait up, Angela".

I smile and hope that they have a great night at the gig they are going to. Conor and I decided that Mum, Mum, or Mother is too difficult to take on at this stage, so I am called Angela by him. He could call me anything and it wouldn't matter. My son. I organise my bag and make sure I have everything with me. I bumped into Clare yesterday when I was with Conor in town. I didn't explain who Conor was and I could see her mind working overtime trying to figure out who he was. "Angela!", she shrieked across Grafton Street. I tried to pretend that I didn't see her but momentarily forgot that she is a force of nature, and she wasn't going to let me go that easily. She filled me in on Matthew's experience in Africa.

"A teacher now, Angela, imagine? Much better than all that horrible financial stuff he was doing here before things got out of hand".

I tried to get away from her, explaining that I was late for my course.

"Your course?", she said.

"Leaving cert", I told her, knowing that I must be the only woman that she knows in her late thirties who hadn't finished her education. She didn't know what to say to say to me but that didn't deter her from writing down Matthew's email address and handing it to me.

"Just in case you want to be in touch", she said and she air-kissed me and continued on her way to meet her ladies for a lunchtime concert in the National Concert Hall. I put Matthews's email address in a bin at the bottom of Grafton Street. I will sit my Leaving Cert next June and who knows what will happen next. University maybe? Or perhaps I'm being a little over-ambitious but as Lucy says, a woman needs to have her dreams. I get the bus into town. I'm too edgy today to drive. It takes me a while to find the office I'm looking for and I get lost a few times. I start to feel

agitated. I think of all the times I did stuff that I didn't want
to do with men who didn't bother to find out my name. I
think of Conor in the home and the years of isolation and
loneliness. But mostly, I think of Francis. And of the life he
could have had. If his innocence was not taken away from
him, by someone who abused his position. I pick up speed
and I find myself on the right road. I stand outside the
offices and see how well-kept they are. I take the stairs
and a girl says to me,

"You are here to see Mr. Reilly?".

"Yes. I certainly am", I reply.

She buzzes through on the intercom and a man says,

"Yes, send her through, Heather".

Heather puts the phone down and tells me to go on
through, that Mr. Reilly is ready to see me. I walk towards
him, and I'm surprised at how ordinary he looks. He is of
average height, bloated and heading towards his late
sixties, I'd say. Near retirement. Thinking he's home and
dry and ready to spend time with the grandchildren whose
photos are in silver frames on his polished walnut desk. I
take a deep breath.

"Take a seat, Angela, did you say?", he says, looking at my

notes on his desk.

"Yes. I'm really hoping you can help me today, Mr. Reilly".

"Well, sweetheart, that's what I am here for. A pretty lady like yourself needn't bother herself worrying about boring things like accounts. You can leave your money worries here with me".

He looks me up and down, his eyes stalling at my cleavage. His tastes must be a bit more varied than I thought. I reach into my bag and remove a few files. I place a copy of the registration number which Conor wrote down many years ago on the desk in front of him. He looks confused.

"I am sorry, sweetheart. I don't know what that is. Sure, look, pass me over your other paperwork, and we'll get to work".

I take a file out. A copy of it has been sent to the police. It's amazing how much information you can find when you have the time and the money. He opens the file, sees the 'Saint Jude' letterhead, and starts to open and close his mouth, in a fish on a hook imitation. I take a metal sheriff's badge out of my bag; the one Conor kept all these years from his boyhood games.

"You never gave him the Sheriff's badge?", I say in a

gentle tone.

"Look, I don't know who the fuck you are or why you are here, but you need to leave my office now", he says, all traces of the flirty gentleman disappeared now.

"Francis? You never gave him the badge. And you said whoever won the game, got the badge. Tut, tut, Mr. Reilly. You really should try to keep your promises".

He stands up abruptly and walks over to me.

"You need to get out of my office now. You stupid bitch", he says.

I watch as his face turns bright red and hope that he doesn't have a heart attack and die on me here. I want him to go to jail first.

"Or what? You'll call the police? Don't worry...", and I glance at my watch,

"...they should be here in about five minutes".

He slumps down on his chair and looks at the photographs of his family in their silver frames. I walk up to him, think of the story Conor told me about being the Lone Ranger on the hill, fashion an imaginary gun from my fingers and say,

"Bang, bang, you're dead".

No Known Relatives

ABOUT THE AUTHOR

Brigid O'Connor is an Irish fiction writer. She was brought up on the north side of Dublin. Her passion for writing was ignited when she won a pound for a poem published in an Irish newspaper, aged 13. Her work has won and been shortlisted for many Irish writing competitions. Her stories have been broadcast nationally on RTÉ Radio 1 - Francis McManus Short Story shortlisted, RTÉ Arena, RTÉ The Book Show and RTÉ Sunday Miscellany.

Her work on RTÉ Lyric FM was broadcast live on national radio at the launch of the programme's anthology in The National Concert Hall. An essay from the show was selected by RTÉ Radio 1 Playback's 'The Best of 2009' and broadcast on the show.

Her poem 'Boy-Man' was published on the New Irish Writing Page/Hennessy Awards Literary Competition in the Irish Independent on 30 April 2011.

She was also shortlisted for the RTE Guide/Penguin Ireland Short Story competition Sept 2013 for a story 'Extra Virgin Olive'.

Her piece, Lololi, was the winner in the Northside Love Stories competition and was read on opening night at the Axis Theatre, Dublin.

Brigid also writes film screenplays and two of her screenplays made it to the top 11% of BBC Writersroom's annual selection process in Drama and Comedy.

She also writes Children's Animation. She was the Development scriptwriter for "Sullivan Sails", working with Distillery Films, which received development funding from Screen Ireland.

She was a contributing writer to children's animated T.V. Series 'MyaGo'. She wrote two episodes - MyaGo 'Camping' and MyaGo 'Basketball'. These two episodes were broadcast on RTÉjr and abroad.

Acknowledgements :

Book cover designed by Arron Inglis.

Photograph via Viktor Forgacs www.Unsplash.com

Extract from 'The Selfish Giant', by Oscar Wilde.

With thanks.

You can connect with me on:

https://twitter.com/WriterBrigid
https://www.linkedin.com/in/brigid-
o%E2%80%99connor-752aba181

No Known Relatives

Printed in Great Britain
by Amazon